CAPITAL

ADORATION

Leigh Jarrett

Published by Steambath Press
An LJ Gay Romance

Paperback published June 2023
ISBN-13: 978-1-998008-10-0

Chapter One |Derek

The evening was uncomfortably warm throughout the city, especially downtown where the concrete and brick held onto the day's heat. There wasn't even a cooling breeze coming off the Pacific Ocean. Mid-summer and Victoria, BC on the west coast of Canada was baking, and most of the old buildings where people were gathered for the night didn't have air-conditioning.

The building up the top of Bastion Square, the site of the original Fort Victoria's log towers, was built with blocks of rough-hewn stone. It had been designed and built by the same man that designed the parliament buildings. Originally, a bank built in a chateau style. It was opulent inside but warm and cozy regardless and made an excellent pub. A great place to gather with friends.

That aside, Derek grunted in irritation.

He hated being the third wheel. And in this case, the ninth wheel. Thursday night and he was out with friends. Friends he'd had for the last fourteen years. He hadn't grown up in the tourist city of Victoria. He'd met the four guys at the table while playing on a men's weekend football team.

Tonight, they were celebrating Jackson's birthday. Everyone had shown up with their wives or girlfriends. Hence, Derek was the ninth wheel. Four couples and him. After three years, it was still an uncomfortable feeling. Being single at a table of couples. Derek and his wife had separated three years ago; divorced after two. He'd been pretty much flying solo since then.

"Another round!" Jackson shouted as he waved at the server.

Things were getting rowdy. Another couple of rounds and the server would be cutting off some of his friends. Derek fiddled with his empty pint glass. He was keeping the drinking to a minimum. He had to work the lunch shift the next day—in the same pub they were sitting in.

It was a fabulous place to work. Everyone was friendly. The servers, the hosts, and the other bartenders. Even the management. He was paid well and the tips were among the best in the city.

Derek hadn't meant to become a career bartender. He'd fallen into it when he was attending university and found it paid better than most jobs he could secure with his four-year Bachelor's degree. Only just legal to drink, he'd started as a bar-back in the pub and worked his way up front. That was nineteen years ago. At thirty-eight, he was one of the oldest employees in the pub.

Chelsea, Jackson's wife leaned toward him and pressed against his shoulder.

"I have someone I want you to meet," she said. "She's new in my office. Divorced five years ago. She's been waiting for the right guy to come along. I think you might be it."

This was a constant. His friends trying to hook him up. He usually took them up on it. What was the harm? An evening spent with a woman they thought suitable. They knew him well, so they were usually pretty spot on. He hadn't been on too many bum dates. Hadn't found the right woman yet, though. Some had been close. Just not anyone he wanted to spend his life with.

"Sure," he said to Chelsea. "Does she know you're talking to me about it?"

"She told me to give you her number." Chelsea opened the contacts on her phone and *shared* it with Derek. His phone dinged. He looked at it.

Laura Crosby.

He'd known a Crosby in high school. An Eric. He wondered if Laura was related.

"Is she from the island?"

"Nope. Just moved from Kelowna."

"What does she do for work in your office."

"Systems analyst."

"No idea what that even is."

"Me either. All I know is she keeps the computer software happy."

"Hobbies?"

"Same as you. Hiking. Walks by the ocean. A bit of kayaking. Snowboarding."

Sounds promising.

Derek didn't need to grill Chelsea about Laura. They'd have a few things to talk about from what she'd told him. They could delve into more topics when they met for their date.

"Let her know, I'll call her tomorrow night."

Chelsea smiled. "Perfect. You're going to love her."

Derek sighed. *Love.* That was something he desperately wanted back in his life again. He was lonely. He needed to find the right woman, though. Someone who would put up with his moods. He often sunk into depression because it always felt like something was missing from his life. That and his past. Some horrors still ran around in his head from when he was a child.

It had been one of the reasons he and his wife had divorced, his depressive episodes. That and she tended to *go shopping*. It had nearly bankrupted them. He was still paying off the debts by way of a consumer proposal for the mountain of bills she had racked up. Three hundred dollars a month for four years. He'd never make that mistake again. Have all the credit cards in his name.

"What do you think, Derek?"

Derek looked up. He hadn't realized how far his mind had wandered. He hadn't been listening to anything his friends were saying.

"Sorry … zoned out. Think about what?"

"Having dental included in the medical services plan."

Jeez, that was a dry topic. How the hell had they arrived at that? He didn't care but decided to weigh in regardless. "Haven't really thought about it. But I wish it was. Save me some money."

And he was all about saving money. Now that his wife was out of the picture, he was building up a nice sum of savings. He wanted to buy an apartment. Another seven years should do it. He needed to be clear of the consumer proposal's hit on his credit rating first. By that time, he'd have a nice down payment. He wouldn't need an outrageous mortgage if he chose the property carefully.

Derek looked over at the bar. Susie was the bartender tonight. They'd tried dating, but whereas he enjoyed outdoor activities, Susie was all about the party life. They'd lasted three weeks. It was a shame. She was gorgeous and funny, and a damned good bartender.

Their server Richard approached the table with the latest round of drinks. Derek leaned back as his Pale Ale was deposited in front of him. Richard was nice to look at. Derek was always glad to see Richard on the schedule for the same days he was working. They had a good banter between them throughout their shift. The guy was a lot of fun to be around.

He pushed down the feelings that surfaced when he thought about Richard. He looked around the table of his friends. They would never accept him if they knew. It was moot, his attraction toward certain men. It wasn't a path he'd ever follow. His attraction to women was enough for him.

Jackson spilled the second beer of the night.

This time it ran off the table onto Derek's lap.

Derek decided he'd had enough for the evening.

He pushed his chair back and rose. "Hey, I'm going to head out." He patted Jackson on the back. "Happy birthday again, man. Remember, you have to work tomorrow."

Jackson laughed. "Might not make it."

"Your choice." Derek waved to everyone as he walked away. "See ya."

The universe aligned or luck was on his side because there was an available cab parked outside the pub. His rental apartment was close to downtown. A five-minute cab ride. He had a car but rarely used it. The occasional trip to an appointment and the warehouse store out in Langford.

Once home, he flicked on the lights inside his apartment door. It was quiet. He missed the patter of feet that used to accompany him coming home. He'd lost his Jack Russell Bingo six months back. It still hurt to think about him. His spleen had ruptured. It had been fast, his demise. One minute, he'd been a happy little dog, the next, Derek was putting him down to end his suffering. Now the apartment was desperately empty.

Derek wandered into the kitchen and poured and downed a glass of water. He didn't want to risk any type of residual effect from the paltry three drinks he had consumed.

He climbed into bed—alone—again.

Maybe Laura would be the woman he was looking for.

He rolled over and fell asleep wondering about it.

The pub was packed. Not unusual for a Friday. Some tables had people taking extended lunch breaks. Most of the rest were likely tourists from the latest cruise ship that had pulled into the city.

All Derek knew; he was crazy busy.

"How are you holding up?" Richard leaned on the bartop as he waited for Derek to make the drinks he had placed for two of his tables. "You're sure flying today."

"I like being busy." Derek pulled a couple of IPAs from the beer tap and set them on the bar mat near Richard. He chanced a glance at Richard. He was classicly handsome. Dark hair. Fabulous eyes. Full lips. And his British accent was icing on a very delicious-looking cake.

"Me too," Richard said. "But it's not the kind of getting busy I like."

Derek grinned. "Still in the honeymoon phase with the new girlfriend, hey?"

"I lucked out. She's amazing. One bonus of working with lots of women. Every once in a while, you stumble across a gem that you click with."

"I've given up dating from the work pool. It makes things

awkward when you break up."

"Then, I suggest you find someone you don't want to break up with."

"Ha. Ha. Wouldn't that be nice … to know ahead of time before you invest all that effort."

Derek finished off two Blackberry Vodka Mojitos by slipping a full mint leaf down the inside of each glass to join the other crushed ones.

Richard lifted each drink onto his tray.

"You're my second favorite person," Richard said. "I hope you find someone." Then he was off, weaving his way toward his section; his tray held high by his muscular arm.

Derek imagined licking it from armpit to wrist.

Stop it.

He wiped down the bar and ripped the next drink order chit off the machine. He rolled his eyes. It was the order for the 20-top upstairs. And just his luck, it wasn't for beer on tap. He was going to have to do some actual work to get these drinks out. He called his bar-back up front. The fresh twenty-year-old kid was going to be learning some drink recipes today.

By the time his shift finished, Derek was exhausted. It was getting close to 8, but he was going to grab some dinner before he went home. He looked at his phone. He almost didn't want to, but he had promised to phone Laura that evening. He slid onto a free barstool and called her number.

"Hello?"

Her voice sounded nice.

"Hey, this is Derek … Chelsea's friend."

"Oh, Derek … great to meet you."

Kind of a weird thing to say. They hadn't met yet.

Maybe she was nervous.

"You too." Long pause. "Are you free tomorrow night? I get off work at 6. We could go out for dinner after that if you'd like."

"That sounds nice. Chelsea told me where you work. I'll meet you there?"

"Perfect."

"Okay … I'll see you then. Bye."

"Right. Yeah. See you then."

Derek pressed the end call button. There was no chemistry. He could tell that already. He had planned to stay on the line for a few minutes. Talk a little bit. The fact she didn't want to spend any time talking to him on the phone concerned him. Maybe she wasn't into this.

He hated walking into a date with an unwilling participant. Sometimes that happened. His friends would pressure someone into going on a date with him. Those dates tended to be civil but short. Sometimes he found them interesting, regardless. He liked meeting new people.

Richard took the bar stool next to him.

"Grabbing dinner?"

Derek nodded. "Yeah, I'm starving."

"Me too. Jessica works tonight, so I might as well stick around for a while." Richard slid back off his stool. "What do you want? I'll key it in."

"Roast beef sounds perfect about now."

"Making that two."

Derek couldn't stop himself. He stared at Richard's perfect ass as he walked away. He averted his eyes. He needed to stop lusting after the guy.

"Nice view." Someone slid in next to him on the stool

Richard had been sitting on. Derek turned to him. His heart skipped a beat. The man sitting beside him was stunning. Piercing gray-blue eyes peering out from a sophisticated, beautiful, and mischievous face. Hair, dark blond. Short on the sides and deliciously long on top. His lips were framed by a gorgeous amount of stubble.

Derek found his voice.

"Don't know what you're talking about."

The guy shrugged. "Okay. Whatever you say. But that is one fine-looking man."

"I hadn't noticed."

"Right." The guy swung his hand up. "I'm Liam."

Derek scowled. He wasn't used to random approaches by anyone in the pub. Sure he talked to people when he was working. That was different. This bordered on invasive.

"Derek," he muttered as he gripped Liam's hand and shook it. No need to be rude. Giving his name wasn't going to hurt.

"You work here, right? I've noticed you before."

"Yeah. I'm a bartender."

"Been doing that long?" Liam asked.

"Sometimes it seems like too long."

"Do you have other dreams when it comes to work?"

Derek furrowed his brow. What was this? A job interview?

Liam continued to study him with genuine, curious eyes. Derek relaxed. Regardless of Liam being so forward, he decided it wouldn't hurt to talk to the guy.

"I wanted to be an addiction counselor. But that meant more school and I just wasn't into it by the time I finished university. This paid well. I stuck with it."

"You could still do it. Be a counselor."

"Nah." Derek shook his head. "Pretty set in my ways."

Liam tipped his head. "No room for anyone else?"

Okay. Kind of personal.

Derek wasn't sure how to answer. He hadn't really thought about it that way. Sure, he liked his solitude but he also had a need for someone special in his life.

"There's room," he answered.

Liam smiled. The action lit up his whole face. "Good to know."

Oh, for fuck's sake.

Derek nearly got up and left. The guy was obviously hitting on him. But his dinner was on the way. And he was finding Liam somewhat intriguing, despite his advances.

He decided to stay put.

Liam leaned on the bartop with one arm, bent at the elbow, and supported his head.

"So, what do you do when you're not hanging around here?" he asked.

"Well … this morning I went kayaking."

Liam sat up straight. "Me too." He waved the bartender over and ordered a gin and tonic. "Where did you go? I was out in Oak Bay today."

"The Gorge."

"Nice. Love it there."

"Do you ever head to Tofino?" Derek asked.

"No. Never been."

"I do a 6-hour day trip up there in Clayoquot Sound. It's stunning."

"Sounds like somewhere I'd like to check out. When are you going next?"

That took Derek by surprise. Was Liam suggesting they go together? He hadn't meant to walk into a date with the guy. He was breathtaking to look at but he didn't date men.

"Not sure."

Liam extended his hand palm up as if to receive something. "Can I give you my number? You can phone me next time you're going maybe … if you're into it."

Derek passed his phone to Liam, not knowing what the hell possessed him to do so. He'd never call the guy. There was no point in having his number.

"Do you mind if I text my phone with yours … so I have your number?" Liam asked.

Derek couldn't stop himself. "Sure, yeah. Go ahead."

That done, Liam rose from his seat. "I'm here with friends. I better get back to them." He gripped Derek's shoulder. "It was nice meeting you."

When Liam released his shoulder, a vacuum opened up around Derek. It was a strange sensation of intense loneliness. He pushed it from his mind. He'd only just met the guy.

He nearly groaned as Liam walked away. Richard had nothing on that guy's ass.

Richard slipped back onto the barstool. "What did Liam want?"

"You know him?"

"Yeah, we used to date."

Derek's eyebrows rose. He'd had no idea Richard was into guys.

"I didn't know you dated men."

Richard shrugged. "Only if someone special comes along." He looked toward the table where Liam was sitting with a group of people. "And that is one special man. Except for when he jammed out on me when things started to get serious. A bit of a habit of his, apparently."

Derek's attention was drawn back to the gorgeous and compelling guy. Liam was chatting with his friends; animated—carefree. "We were talking about kayaking."

"Yeah, he's big into that." Richard pushed a napkin-wrapped packet of cutlery toward Derek. "So, are you going to go out with him? I'm assuming he asked."

Richard's girlfriend Jessica slipped their plates of roast beef dinner in front of them, kissed Richard on the cheek, then went about her way.

"He suggested we go out to Tofino together."

"And what did you say?" Richard took a scoop of mashed potatoes and stuffed his mouth with it. A stray drip of gravy decorated his bottom lip.

Again—the licking thought popped into Derek's mind.

"I don't date guys," Derek said.

"Oh … sorry. I thought you did."

"What would make you think that?"

"I've seen more than a few hungry stares coming off you when a hot guy comes in."

That was unexpected news. Derek hadn't realized he'd been doing that. Especially, noticeably. He needed to get that in check. People catching on at work was the last thing he needed.

Derek squirmed in his seat. "I appreciate men. Doesn't mean I want to date them."

That was an admission he was willing to make.

"Maybe you should. Liam is certainly a good starting place."

"Why do you say that? That I should start with Liam."

Richard's face softened. "He's warm and caring. And he's an attentive and gentle lover. He's like no one I've ever dated before. It's been a year and I still miss him."

Derek shook his head. "Not interested." He sliced up his meat and mixed it with the potatoes. It was a habit from childhood. The cheap meat they had eaten had been so tough it had needed moisture from the whipped, milky potatoes to make it palatable.

He stole a second look at Liam before he took his first mouthful of the comfort food. Liam glanced up and caught him staring. The wink Liam gave him went straight to his cock.

He was fooling himself if he thought he wasn't interested.

Chapter Two | Liam

It was unlike him—to approach a guy like that. Chat him up with the intention of making his attraction known. He'd seen Derek working behind the bar on many occasions. He often looked sad. Liam wondered what was behind that brooding expression. He found himself tempted to peel back those layers he knew were there. Find the core of the man. Maybe bring him a little joy.

He had no idea if Derek was gay or not. He certainly had eyes for Richard. But then, that was understandable. Even a straight guy would notice the beauty of the guy. Plus, Richard was pure sunshine. He'd been at odds when he broke up with him.

Derek was rugged in appearance. Dark hair and stubble. Gentle brown, tentative eyes. Broad shoulders—trim waist. Built like an American footballer. Liam sipped his drink.

He wouldn't mind being tackled by him.

"Okay, stop staring." His friend Daniel nudged him. "He's got hot and handsome down but I know for a fact he used to date one of the female bartenders."

Liam pursed his lips, then frowned.

Pity.

He continued his assessment of Derek. The guy was watching him again. Maybe his sexuality wasn't fixed. Derek refocused on his dinner. The next time Derek looked at him, Liam winked at him. The complexity of the reaction on Derek's face was adorable—and telling.

The man was obviously at odds with his attraction to men. He didn't need that in his life. He only dated men that were comfortable with who they were. Out and proud men that weren't afraid to show affection in public. When he dated a woman, that problem never came up. Women tended to like that extra display of affection. He liked being able to hold hands with whomever he dated.

"Don't go there," Daniel said.

"Not planning on it."

There was no future for them.

Liam used the little straw in his drink to stir it. The ice cubes clinked in his glass. Then why couldn't he take his eyes off the man? And why couldn't the man take his eyes off him?

He needed to go.

"I'm out of here. Cover my drinks. I'll pay you back." Liam slid out of the booth. He took one last look at Derek before he headed out the door. He was going to be on his mind for a while.

Derek caught Liam staring.

Damn, the intense longing carried in Derek's gaze was cock stirring.

He ducked through the door outside. The whole way down the sidewalk to his apartment in Chinatown, Derek's obvious desire was playing on repeat.

The little seafood restaurant upstairs of a heritage building was one of the best in the city. Their mussels in white wine were to die for. The ambiance was cozy. He'd had many a date there.

Men and women. He just let his attraction guide him.

Liam looked across the table. He was on his second date with Pamela. She was fun to be with. Their conversations were light and friendly.

Friendly.

Yeah, that's where this was going. There was no spark. He had no desire to take her home. Unless she was into it. They both knew this wasn't developing into anything special.

Maybe she'd be into a friends-with-benefits arrangement.

He clung tight to his fork as none other than the man invading his every thought appeared in the dining area. Derek was wearing a casual cotton, summer-weight suit. He looked absolutely drool-worthy. The woman he was with was pretty. A flattering, flowing floral dress swished as she walked. It was obvious it was a first date. They weren't speaking and they both looked nervous.

Then Derek caught sight of Liam.

A yearning nod is what Liam got from Derek.

Liam nodded back, returning the sentiment. His cock stirred at the thought of kissing those stern lips and finding his way beneath Derek's challenging exterior.

He cleared the thought from his mind.

There was no way he was even going to attempt that. He had no doubt Derek was interested. But would Derek be open to following his attraction? It was highly unlikely.

He and Pamela ordered another bottle of wine and finished their dinner. He was stalling. Watching Derek lift food to his lips was doing delicious things to his insides.

"Want to get out of here?" Pamela asked. "Go

somewhere private."

Liam smiled at her. She was a cute and sultry blonde. He hadn't slept with a woman for a while. He'd been on a kick of men recently. Her invitation was a welcome one.

"Your place?" he asked.

"Either. I'm just across the bridge. We could walk."

Her place was best. Something in him didn't want Pamela to come back to his place tonight. She might stay the night and she wasn't the person he wanted to wake up to.

He took one last furtive glance at Derek before heading down the stairs. Derek and his date still weren't talking much. Liam smiled. Derek was striking out. It brought him a sense of relief.

Liam and Pamela walked arm and arm across the bridge. The trip was full of laughter and teasing. Pamela had made note of the fact he was staring at *some guy* in the restaurant.

She thought it was hot that he slept with men.

Once inside her apartment, Liam pressed Pamela to the wall and descended on her mouth. She tasted like the wine they had been drinking. And something so much sweeter.

His cock thickened wondering what the rest of her would taste like.

He took a break from her lips.

"This is a no-strings thing, right?" he asked. He needed to make sure Pamela wasn't thinking they were moving into relationship territory. He wouldn't sleep with her if that was the case.

"None at all," Pamela answered. "The only way we're clicking is sexual."

Green light.

Liam started with her top, removed it, and kissed every piece of exposed skin. Her bra found its way onto the floor next. Every move after was designed to bring her incredible pleasure. He always put his lovers first. She'd come away from this experience feeling respected and revered.

Because she was.

He slipped off her skirt.

Liam rolled over in bed—his bed. He'd nipped out of Pamela's around 2 in the morning. She'd given him a long, sensuous kiss. A promise of more. That he could handle. She was a responsive, voracious lover. He would sleep with her again in a heartbeat.

Just like someone else.

Dammit.

He slapped his hand over his eyes.

Derek had slipped into his mind. The unattainable man was under his skin. He wondered what kind of lover he would be. Commanding—submissive. Kinky—vanilla. He imagined the sounds he'd make. His cock swelled. He reached beneath the covers for it—and dealt with it.

Forty seconds later, his hand sticky, Liam made his way to the shower. He took his time under the hot water. He wasn't working today. The plan was to head out onto the ocean.

Derek had enjoyed The Gorge. It put him in the mind to go there. It wouldn't be a hard paddle, but it would be a picturesque one. The waterway was only six kilometers long and stretched from Selkirk Trestle to the head of Portage Inlet. He could stretch the trip out to an hour and a half if he doubled back for part of it. He'd launch somewhere in the middle.

After his shower, he slipped into a plain, red t-shirt and board shorts. He hauled his kayak out from his storage unit and loaded it onto his car. It was cumbersome to load it onto the rack, but it was worth it. There was nothing like being out on the water. He'd grown up on Vancouver Island. Ocean water ran in his veins from the time he was a child.

Liam pulled into the parking lot and performed the entire exercise in reverse. It wasn't until he slipped the kayak into the water that he felt at peace. He stepped in and pushed off. He'd head to Selkirk Trestle first, then enjoy the entire trip to the open ocean.

A figure paddling in the opposite direction off to his right caught his attention. He dug his paddle in and changed course. He soon caught up to the leisurely pace of his target.

Liam pulled up to the starboard of Derek's kayak.

"Hey. Didn't think you'd be out this way again so soon."

"Enjoyed it the other day." Derek placed his paddle across the cockpit. "One of my favorites when I'm being lazy. No strong currents to fight."

"That's what I needed today. Had a long strenuous night."

"Your date?"

Okay, Liam had dropped that hint on purpose. Maybe Derek wouldn't be as scared of him if he knew he slept with women—too. "Yeah ... firmly in the friend zone, though."

Derek's brow furrowed. He'd confused him. That hadn't been his intention. He'd been trying to ease Derek's anxiety around him. Not ramp it up.

"You have sex with your friends?" Derek asked.

"Just the special ones." Liam had an arrangement with

several friends. His friend Daniel being one of them. He preferred it to a relationship. Relationships always turned messy and tenuous. One tiny thing could upset the whole balance. When his heart stirred and started to become involved, he would end it. A clean break was better than a broken heart.

Derek huffed and turned his gaze toward the water in front of them.

"Paddle with me?" he asked.

"Love to."

They didn't speak for the next thirty minutes. Just enjoyed the scenery. Liam kept a few strokes behind so he could watch Derek's broad, muscular shoulders paddle. He could imagine gripping them as he drilled Derek from behind. The image stirred far too much interest in his cock.

"I'm going to Tofino next Thursday," Derek said. He slowed until Liam caught up. "I could give you a ride if you want to come with me. We'd have to leave at 6 in the morning."

Liam mentally flipped through his work schedule. He was working Thursday, but he could easily get someone to take his shift. The working shortage was finally starting to ease in the therapy rooms of the cancer clinic. It gave everyone some breathing room instead of being run off their feet. Even busy, he loved his job as a chemotherapy technician. It was extremely rewarding work.

"I can be ready to go at 6. I'll text you my address."

He was playing with embers. He knew that. A little breath of air in the right direction would lead to combustion. He'd need to contain any potential gusts. Derek was off-limits.

The rest of the paddle was mostly quiet. There was a spat of racing each other which led to some laughter. It was nice to see Derek smile. Even though the smile didn't reach his eyes.

Derek paddled ahead.

To put a smile on that man's face that came from his soul could be a man's sole mission in life. But he wasn't that man. He just hoped someone would be that person for Derek someday.

At 6 on Thursday morning, Liam was ready. According to the weather forecast, the elements looked like they were going to cooperate. They'd had seventy-six days of straight sunshine but Tofino could be a bit unpredictable when it came to weather. It was open ocean all the way to Japan on that side of the island. Storms often swept in without much notice.

He yanked on his body-hugging summer wetsuit. It left little to the imagination. Even though it was sweltering hot out, if he ended up in the cold sea water, he'd need the extra protection. That and it was impossible not to get wet. He packed a change of clothes into a backpack.

"I bought coffee," Derek said as they loaded Liam's kayak onto Derek's car. "Figured you were a black coffee guy. Snagged some cream and sugar in case I was wrong."

"No ... black is good."

Liam slipped into the passenger seat. Derek took a seat beside him and started the car. It was well-loved—the car. Worn dash and seats. He just hoped it had air-conditioning. That question was answered with a rush of cold air. He looked down at the coffees.

"Which one is mine?"

"Take your pick. They're both black."

Liam popped the tab on one of the coffees and pressed it into place to stay open. He took a tentative sip. It was still scalding hot. He set it back in the cup holder.

Derek pulled away from the curb and they started what would be a 4-hour drive.

"Can you open mine?" Derek asked.

"It's too hot to drink." Liam set the tab open on Derek's coffee. "That'll help to cool it off." He settled in his seat and watch the scenery go by. They went from the Victoria cityscape, over the Malahat, to stretches of highway with spurts of small towns. He'd never been beyond Parksville before. One of his foster families had taken him camping there once. He had tried to run off. He had been bounced off to another foster home after that. Deemed unmanageable.

That had been the story for the next six years until he turned eighteen. He could still picture the look on the face of his foster mom when she caught him in bed with a guy. That had been in grade eleven. He'd been turned out. Sent to his last foster home. It had been brutal there.

He rubbed his hands together. They'd tried to strap the gayness out of him. It had certainly turned him off dating guys for a while. That's when he'd discovered he liked women as well.

"You grow up in Victoria?" Derek asked.

"Yeah. You?"

"Port Alberni."

Liam must have made a funny face because Derek laughed. He reached for his coffee. "It wasn't that bad. My grandparents had a little piece of property. Was fun to run around on as a kid."

"You visited there a lot?"

Derek shook his head. "No. My grandparents raised me." Liam noticed Derek grip the steering wheel tighter. "My parents died in a car crash when I was five."

Liam looked down at his hands. Suddenly his treatment in foster care didn't seem that bad. Even though his mother wanted nothing to do with him, she was still alive last he checked. His brother kept in contact with her. Reported back to him after he'd visited with her.

"I'm sorry. That must have been devastating," Liam said.

"To be honest … I don't remember much about them. Too young, I guess."

"Still." Liam fiddled with his coffee. "Hey, can I ask you a question?"

"Maybe."

"Every time I see you, you seem sad."

"That's not a question."

"It's implied."

Derek lifted his cup and took a sip. He drove one-handed down the next stretch of road. They were entering the Cathedral Grove area where many of the cedar trees were eight hundred years old. It was a magnificent temperate rainforest Liam had never been through before.

Liam was awestruck as they drove past the entrances to the park. It was now on his list of places to visit in the future. Or maybe after they finished kayaking.

Derek hadn't answered his question and he wasn't going to push him. Two hours later, they were in Tofino. Liam nearly stumbled as he stepped through the trees onto the deserted beach, the sight was so overwhelming. He'd never seen anything like it. Pictures—sure. But that didn't touch on the reality of the place. He adjusted his kayak and stood in place, staring.

An expanse of wet, grey, sandy beach as far as the eye could see. Rocky outcrops. Cedars perched atop many. Rumbling waves in the distance. Derek had brought them to a protected area where they'd be able to paddle out from. He followed Derek out to the water.

Transcendent; that's the word that kept coming to mind as they paddled their way along the coastline. He felt like he was experiencing something otherworldly, it was so mythical. Like they had stepped back in time to when the earth was pristine. He half expected to see dinosaurs.

"Look!" Derek pointed out to the open ocean.

In the distance, a pod of grey whales breached the surface of the water with absolute majesty. Close by, sea lions kept popping their little faces out of the water to check them out. A pod of dolphins made an appearance, swimming alongside their kayaks for quite a distance; curious.

Hauling those kayaks out of the water after the 6-hour journey was exhausting but Liam felt exhilarated. This had been the trip of a lifetime. He was so grateful Derek had taken the chance on a potential friendship and asked him along with him.

They dug their backpacks out of the back of the car. Trying to strip a damp wetsuit off was never fun. After unzipping each other, they both sat on the bumper of the car and went to work.

Liam chanced a look after Derek pulled the wetsuit off his feet. Derek's bare cock was tight against his balls, the cold water contracting everything. Liam nearly hummed aloud.

He would gladly take on that challenge.

Warming up Derek's cock with his mouth.

But he'd promised himself, he wouldn't touch—or engage.

Their dry clothes on, Derek slammed the back hatch closed. Liam offered to drive back and Derek was all over that. He was asleep within minutes of them starting home.

Liam kept glancing over at him. He couldn't help imagining Derek asleep beside him like that. So peaceful. His worries set aside after a night of lovemaking.

He sighed. It wasn't to be. Unless Derek miraculously came to terms with his sexuality and embraced it, he wasn't going to come within a paddle's length of him.

Chapter Three | Derek

For most of the trip home, Derek took advantage of the quiet and slept. Every once in a while, he would open an eye to see if Liam was still okay to drive. One of those times, he'd caught Liam glancing over at him. There was such tenderness and concern in his eyes, it was startling.

No one had ever looked at him like that.

It made him feel warm inside.

He closed his eyes and enjoyed the hum of the car engine. Their excursion had been epic. The wildlife had come out in full force. The expressions on Liam's face had been heart-stopping. So much wonder and appreciation. He was glad he'd asked Liam to come along.

The car slowed. Stopping and starting at lights.

"We're almost at my place," Liam said.

Derek righted himself in his seat. He'd been leaning against the window. He yawned and stretched out his back. He needed to wake up fully so he could drive the short distance home.

Liam pulled up to the curb outside his apartment. He turned off the engine and handed the keys to Derek. "Give me a hand with my kayak?"

"Absolutely."

They both crawled out of the car and hoisted Liam's kayak off the roof rack. There was a struggle maneuvering it. Derek's shoulders were already killing him. Liam's had to be the same. They were both going to feel this in the morning. What he needed right now was a hot shower.

An image of Liam standing naked beneath a shower flicked through his mind.

Stop it.

Liam shouldered his kayak.

"Thanks for today. I really appreciate you asking me along."

"Sure, yeah." Derek scrubbed the back of his neck. He'd enjoyed hanging out with the guy. Would suggesting another adventure send the wrong message? This still wouldn't be a date.

He decided he didn't care what signal it sent.

"We should do it again," Derek said.

And there it was, that stunning smile that lit up Liam's face.

"I'd love to," Liam answered. "Text me when and where, and I'll make it work."

"I'll do that … I have your number."

Liam shifted onto one hip. "Hey, do you belong to the kayaking association?"

"No, never heard of it."

"We meet once a month. Talk about our trips." Liam took a couple of steps toward Derek. "We're meeting tomorrow night for dinner. You should come."

That sounded interesting. He could get on board with meeting a bunch of kayaking enthusiasts. Plus, it would be a chance to hang out with Liam again.

"I'm not working tomorrow," Derek said. "Works for me. Text me the details, okay?"

"Okay. Good." Liam extended his arm and gave Derek a

fist pump. "Thanks again."

Derek nodded and walked back to the driver's side of the car. Before he opened the door, he took a moment and watched Liam walk away. His ass really was incredible.

Carnal thoughts invaded his mind.

Again—with the licking.

Stop it.

When he pulled into his parking lot, he was so ready to head inside and hit the shower to relieve the pressure building in his cock. But he had to unload the kayak first. The delay almost drove him insane. Finally, in the shower, he stroked and came hard with Liam on his mind.

He gripped the wall.

The unstoppable urge to do so terrified him.

The kayaking association had booked a meeting room in a restaurant just outside downtown. Derek was surprised by the number of people gathered for the dinner. Twenty—at least.

Derek spotted Liam on the far side of the large table. He had an empty chair beside him. It thrilled him to think Liam had been saving it for him. That he wanted to ensure they sat together.

"Hey," Derek said as he slipped in beside Liam.

"Glad you made it." Liam passed a menu to Derek. "I already know what I'm having."

"What did you pick?"

"Snapper with a creamy caper sauce and rice."

"Sounds great." Derek scanned through the menu. It was pricey. He looked through the appetizers. Maybe there was something there that would satisfy him. The prices, though.

He may as well order a full dinner. "I'm feeling like a burger."

He could see Liam biting his tongue; a teasing comment dancing on his lips. It made Derek smile. Things weren't completely easy between them … yet. With time, it would come.

The meeting was very informative and interesting. Once they were settled, there was some business to get out of the way first, then people shared details of their latest kayaking trips. Liam took a turn to speak and relayed the breathtaking experience they'd had together. He was quick to comment that the company greatly improved the entire trip. People nodded their agreement.

Liam pressed his shoulder to Derek's. Derek's entire body buzzed in response to the contact. "I really did enjoy going with you," Liam whispered.

Derek could barely breathe. He managed a "So did I."

He could sense Liam hesitating beside him.

"I'm looking forward to what comes next," Liam said at last.

Okay, that was definitely a pass. It didn't deter him, though. Derek already had another trip floating around in his mind. He had no intention of going alone. "Next Tuesday … Oak Bay."

"What time?"

"Early. 7. I have to work at 1."

"I'll be there. Text me where you want to meet."

Liam moved away. And again, that damned vacuum opened up around Derek. This time, his heart skipped a beat. It was going to be difficult to maintain a friendship with Liam if he kept lusting after him. He had no idea how achievable subduing that impulse would be, but if it meant he could spend more time with Liam, he'd lock down every bit of attraction he had for him.

They ate in silence, listening to the conversations around them. A couple of times, Liam nudged him and snorted when someone said something amusing.

They made quick work of their meals.

"How was your burger?" Liam asked.

"Good. Your snapper?"

"Great." Liam leaned back as someone took their plates. "Now that we've determined the food was good, tell me more about growing up in Port Alberni. Can't imagine there was much to do."

"It was all right. I was a bit of a terror as a teenager."

"Weren't we all?"

"Yeah. Staying out late. Coming home drunk."

"Check and check," Liam replied.

"So, you drove your parents crazy, hey."

Liam hesitated and frowned. Derek wished he could take it back, the comment. He had obviously landed on a touchy subject.

"I grew up in foster care," Liam said.

Derek hadn't expected that. He'd never met anyone who had been raised in foster care.

"I'm sorry. That must have been tough."

"I survived, that's the main thing. Consolation prize, my university was free."

"Were you able to stay with one family?"

Liam shook his head. "No. I was too much of a handful. Plus, it was pretty obvious I was queer. Two things most foster families don't want to deal with. I moved around a lot."

"And they would just do that … pass you on?"

"Seven homes in twelve years."

Derek was stunned at how anyone could keep moving a child from family to family like that. No stability. No consistency. No love.

How on earth had Liam grown up without love in his life?

The urge to hug him was overwhelming.

Hug him—and hold him.

Kiss him.

But, of course, he didn't.

The meeting finished, and back in his car, Derek leaned his head on the headrest. He was kidding himself if he thought he could put his desire for Liam on a shelf.

It was more than lust. Richard had been right. Liam was a warm and caring guy. But there was also so much hurt there. He needed to know more about him.

Tuesday wasn't going to come soon enough.

The morning was drizzly with rain but that wasn't going to deter them. They set out from the shore toward the Chatham and Discovery Islands. It was a 2km paddle and the winds made it difficult but once they were there, it was worth it. There were nooks and crannies everywhere on the rocky islands to explore. Derek had never been out that way before, but Liam was familiar.

They rounded an outcrop and Liam pulled up on the shore and climbed out.

"There are trails up this way."

Derek hauled his kayak out of the water next to Liam's

and followed him inland up a steep incline and through an opening in the trees. He had to scramble to keep up.

Liam was right. There were trails. It was nice to get off the water for a few minutes and give his shoulders a rest. Liam headed off the trail and into the trees.

Derek found him rolling a log, then taking a seat on it. Liam picked up a stick and started poking around in what looked like an old fire pit.

"Do people camp here?" Derek asked.

Liam turned and smiled at him. "Some of my best nights as a teenager were out here."

"Building campfires?"

"Creating some heat, to be sure." Liam tossed his stick into the trees. "A buddy from school used to let me borrow his two-person kayak. Went *camping* with a lot of guys."

Derek had so many questions about that.

"You've always known you were interested in guys?" he asked.

"Since kindergarten. Came home telling my mom I wanted to marry *Johnny.*"

Derek sat beside Liam. He'd been interested in *Johnny* when he was a kid. But he'd been more interested in *Jane.* "You're bisexual."

"When I feel attraction toward someone, I don't question it. Gender is never a deciding factor."

To have that kind of freedom … Derek was envious.

"What do your friends think?"

"I've never hidden it. People don't stick around if it bothers them."

"Are you're all right with that?"

"Why wouldn't I be? It's my life … not theirs."

If only it was that easy. Derek looked up at the swaying trees. The wind had picked up. "We should get going before the weather changes."

"Yeah." Liam touched Derek's arm as he stood. "We should camp here sometime. I have all the gear. Tent, sleeping bags. We'd have to haul firewood over in the kayaks, though."

And where would that lead? Sleeping in the same tent.

Derek didn't trust himself.

"Maybe."

Liam caught his gaze and held it. "Think about it."

Derek turned back toward the trail. He'd be thinking about it all right. In bed—in the shower. He'd be adding sleeping beneath the stars with Liam; the tent smelling of sex to his fantasies.

Back across the inlet, they hauled their kayaks onto the rocky beach. The waves had been choppier than they would have liked. It had been hard going, paddling through it. Derek's shoulders and biceps were burning, but it was a good burn. He liked pushing his body. It crowded out the thoughts and memories in his head. All the terrifying things he wished he could forget.

"I'm not going to be able to lift my arms for a week," Liam joked.

"I hear you. Work this afternoon is going to be brutal."

Liam set his kayak down. "Hey, when do you finish work today? We could grab a drink afterward. We don't get a chance to talk much while we're out on the water."

Derek lifted his kayak onto his shoulder. It was a dangerous idea but it was an expected progression. They knew very little about each other. It would be nice to talk more over a drink.

"Usually around 8."

"Should I come by your work?"

"Yeah, we can head out from there."

"Sounds perfect." Liam bit his bottom lip as he studied Derek. Then he licked his lips—slow. Derek nearly groaned. The look on his face must have given him away because Liam smiled at him with more than a knowing glance. They stood and stared at each other for much too long.

Derek's heart thundered in his chest.

He had no doubt … tonight's drink was a date.

Derek was sweating, he was so nervous. There was every possibility, he had misinterpreted the signals. The camping invitation. The few moments on the beach. As he pulled the next beer off the tap, he pictured Liam's tongue sweeping across his lips. That had been a deliberate test. To see how he'd react. He'd either passed or failed depending on where you stood.

The score. Friendship—zero. Attraction—one.

It was nearly 8. He checked the hostess area up front as he worked. Any minute now, his possible, probable date was going to walk through that door.

Date.

How the hell had he gotten there?

The next time he turned to face the bartop, Liam was perched on a stool in front of him. He was wearing a white shirt with thin golden threads, unbuttoned to expose his tanned chest. His sleeves were rolled up. The broad white bands accentuated his muscular forearms.

He was stunning.

"Hey, gorgeous," Liam whispered to him.

His cock thickened.

No misinterpreted signals.

This was a date.

"I'll just be another minute. Can I get you a drink while you're waiting?"

"I can hold out until you're ready."

Heat crept up Derek's cheeks to his ears. There was an obvious double meaning there. Liam knew this was all new to him and he wasn't going to push him.

"I just need to clock out."

"I'll be right here."

Derek ran straight into Richard on his way to the staff room. Richard had come up the stairs from the kitchen. He was flustered. Problems with an order, according to what he was mumbling.

"You okay?" Derek asked.

"It was a simple request. No mayonnaise. The table gave me shit." Richard crossed his arms. He closed his eyes and counted to 10. He exhaled and breathed easier. "Are you off?"

"Yeah. Going for a drink with Liam."

No point in hiding it. Richard was going to catch sight of Liam waiting at the bar. There was no other reason he'd be sitting there without a drink in his hand.

"Date?"

Derek sighed. "Might be."

Richard slapped his shoulder. "Good for you. Enjoy him." There was a hint of sadness in Richard's eyes. He gave Derek a small smile, then turned and headed for the dining room.

What on earth had happened between them? It was obvious Richard had been in love with Liam. Had Liam really just cut him loose? Did he even want to go out with this guy if he had?

He shut his locker.

One date didn't mean they had to take it further. It might not even go well. Although, he doubted that. They'd been having a lot of fun with each other.

He felt a wave of elation that buried his anxiety as he approached the bar area. The beautiful man waiting there was waiting for him. He took a deep breath and joined him. They decided on a busy restaurant up Trounce Alley. It was crowded but the energy was great. They found a couple of vacant barstools amidst the fray of buzzing conversation. They ordered a couple of drinks.

Derek leaned toward Liam. "Tell me more about your job."

Liam tipped his head. "Not much to tell. Patients come to us to get their cancer treatments. Some of them are there every day. We request the meds and then administer them. Keep them as comfortable as possible. The amount of pain they're in sometimes … it's heartbreaking."

"That sounds brutal. How do you cope?"

"We get some decent breaks between blocks of shifts. It's hard, though. Many patients don't survive. Watching people fade away before your eyes—it does a number on your head."

"Why do you do it?"

"How could I not? We're the only hope these people have. We administer the thing that could cure them. If I could save them all, I would gladly give up everything."

Derek leaned back in his seat. The depth of emotion Liam had poured out was overwhelming. To dedicate your life to try and save people's lives … was an honorable path.

It suited Liam. He wouldn't have expected anything less from him.

"And here I am, a lowly bartender."

"Don't do that." Liam touched his wrist. "Even a lowly bartender has his place in the whole scheme of things. In some ways, you provide as much comfort to people as I do."

Liam withdrew his hand. The absence of it created a hole. Derek almost reached for Liam's leg beneath the bartop. Just to touch him … to feel his warmth.

"Tell me more about your grandparents," Liam said.

Derek shrugged. "They did their best. They didn't have the money to raise a hungry kid. We went without a lot. Kids used to tease me about my clothes and how skinny I was."

Liam's eyebrows raised. "You've certainly filled in nicely now."

A rush of crimson colored Derek's cheeks. "Things got better when I moved out and started working at the bar. Been there eighteen years now."

"Dedicated employee."

"Dedicated or unmotivated … not sure which."

"Well, I think you look delicious behind the bar."

The blush reached his ears; itchy. For a second, he'd forgotten they were on a date. He felt so comfortable with Liam. The casual drink was no different from hanging out with a buddy.

Except Liam wanted more from him.

They wouldn't be going there tonight. He wasn't ready

for that. Didn't know if he'd ever be ready for that. He'd never slept with a man before. He had no idea what to expect.

He didn't even know if he'd like it.

Chapter Four | Liam

It was agonizing. The thought of waiting for Derek to conquer his nerves and come to terms with his sexuality. But Liam wasn't going to rush him. He had a feeling Derek would be worth it. That he'd discover something wonderful underneath all that angst and sadness.

"You said you grew up in foster care," Derek said.

"From the time I was six." Liam twirled his glass on the bar top. How much to tell. He wasn't sure. He took a sip of his drink. He felt close to the man beside him. He would share part of it.

"My mom was a drug addict."

"I'm sorry."

"Don't be. It was her decision."

"You were taken from her?"

Liam shook his head. "No … she gave me up."

Derek's hand came to rest on Liam's knee. "Jeezus, Liam. I'm sorry."

"Seriously, don't be sorry … it's just the way it was."

Liam set his hand on top of Derek's and wrapped his fingers around it. Derek lasted a few seconds before he pulled away. That simple action of withdrawing yanked the floor out from beneath him. He wanted this man so badly. To have Derek hold him and keep the world at bay.

"Do you have any siblings?" Derek asked.

That was the other half of the story.

"Can we talk about this some other time? This is supposed to be fun? I didn't take an incredible risk and imply a date to talk about depressing stuff."

Derek smiled. "So, this *is* a date."

"Does that scare you?"

"A little bit. I've never been on a date with a man before."

"Not even a little one?" Liam asked.

"Nope. My life has been filled with women."

"Mmm … women are nice. They taste good."

"That they do," Derek said.

"Men taste pretty good too." Liam reached for Derek's knee. He gripped and caressed it.

Derek didn't pull away.

"I bet you taste good," Liam continued.

"Slow it down, Liam ... please."

Liam sighed and released Derek's knee. "I'll go as slow as you want. But can you do me a favor and stop looking so scrumptious? You're going to do me in."

Derek laughed. Softly. But he laughed—and it almost reached his eyes.

Liam had promised himself, he wouldn't be the guy to take on the challenge of breaking down Derek's defenses, but here he was. The man had crawled beneath his guard rails.

He finished his drink.

Truth was, he'd carved holes in those guard rails to let the guy in.

"So, you've got a bachelor's in what … social work?" Liam asked.

"Took me five years."

"I considered that. The whole addictions counseling thing. Hit a little too close to home."

"Yeah, I would say so." Derek kept his attention on

Liam. "Do you snowboard?"

Liam appreciated that Derek didn't launch into a line of questioning about his mom and how she had come to give him up. Winter sports, though. It made Liam nervous that Derek saw them hanging out when the winter snow hit. That was still months and months away.

Maybe he should abandon this quest before anyone got hurt.

End it now.

"Liam?"

Derek's soft brown eyes were watching him; yearning for reassurance. Against what his mind was screaming, Liam's heart swelled with anticipation of more time spent with the incredible man before him. He needed to stick around. To see if the light could ever reach those eyes.

"Snowboarding. Absolutely."

Derek smiled. "I've often toyed with the idea of buying a place up at Mt. Washington. I spend so much time on the slopes. Hotels get kind of expensive."

"I have a place." Liam took a sip of his drink. He'd bought the condo earlier in the year. Once he drove out to Mt. Washington, it was best to stay for a few days. Or a week if he had enough vacation time he could use. Snowboarding was his winter passion.

"Really?" Derek nearly laughed. It was obvious, he was excited by the prospect of having a place to stay on the mountain despite this only being their first date. Derek was oblivious to the reality of where their relationship would be by the time winter rolled around.

Liam stared at his hands. "Yeah, just bought it at the end of last season. Paid a decent price because we were moving into late spring."

Surely, Richard had told him. He was no good at long-term. He and Derek had strayed away from the friend zone. Their time together was limited now.

When Liam looked up, Derek's brow was furrowed.

"I'm sorry," Derek said. "I didn't mean to jump ahead."

Liam shook his head. "No. You're fine. Let's just enjoy each other for now, though, okay?"

"Okay." Derek lifted the menu. "Are you hungry?"

Awesome. Change in direction. "Yes. Famished."

"I hear the garlic prawns and seafood linguine are amazing."

"One of each? We can swap some?"

"Great idea."

While they waited for their food, they switched to talking about kayaking locations. A couple of places, they made plans to go together. Others, solo.

Their server slid their food in front of them. They shifted half their portions of food to each other's plates. It was a messy endeavor but it got Derek smiling and laughing.

The slivers of joy looked good on him.

So good, Liam wanted to touch Derek's lips. Kiss them—and have them kiss him back. Liam released a long exhalation.

"Are you all right?" Derek asked.

"To be honest, I was thinking about kissing you."

Derek's eyebrows rose. "Right here? Now?"

"No … after. Once we're out of here."

Derek's eyes searched his. Looking for what, Liam wasn't sure. He appeared to come to a decision. "Then, I think we should finish up."

The implications ran a shiver up Liam's spine.

Maybe the cogs of Derek's sexuality were starting to turn.

They finished their food and drink, paid their bills, then headed out into Trounce Alley. It had a constant stream of people, but Liam found a dark spot by a brick wall and leaned against it.

"So, what now?" Liam asked.

He had promised not to push. He was going to let Derek come to him.

Derek wandered toward him, then came in close. He cupped Liam's face in one hand and breathed across his chin. The first meeting of their lips was gentle. The next was desperate and ravenous. Each one after that escalated their desire. Derek used his hips to pin Liam to the wall and ground against him, his cock swelling. Derek groaned and increased the pressure. The kiss made Liam dizzy with need. He clung to Derek not wanting to ever let him go.

They parted to catch a breath and Derek stepped back. He looked dazed. He hadn't expected his body to react like that. Liam could see it in his eyes.

"Derek ... are you all right?"

Derek stepped back further. "I'm sorry. I need to go home."

Liam jogged the short distance as Derek turned and began to walk away. He grabbed Derek's arm. "Please don't run. Talk to me."

Derek spun on him. "What's there to talk about? I can't do this."

"I get it. You're scared." Liam clung to Derek's arm. "Let's not blow things up over a kiss."

Derek removed Liam's hand from his arm. "I felt that kiss in my damned toes."

"Why is that so wrong?"

"I don't date men."

"You just did. And we had a good time."

Derek heaved out a sigh. "Can we go back to being friends?"

"After a kiss like that?" Liam shook his head. "I don't think I can do that."

"So … this is it for us?"

Liam felt like his world was collapsing. It was more than desire he was feeling for Derek. In his mind, it was like a Rubik's cube had snapped into place; all of the colors lined up where they were supposed to be. They'd made a deep connection so much more than friends.

"I don't want it to be finished between us," Liam said.

"Then how do we move forward?"

"By taking a step back."

"What would that look like?"

"Kayaking and spending time together with no pressure to make things physical." As difficult as that would be. "But keeping in mind we're doing those things as more than friends."

Derek was hesitating. His posture spoke volumes. He kept looking away over his shoulder. He was still considering walking away.

Please don't walk away from me.

Derek stared at him and his features softened. "Next Sunday at 8 am. Thetis Lake?"

Liam released the breath he'd been holding. "I'll be there."

Sunday morning was beautiful and sunny. It would be a leisurely paddle around the lake. They'd be able to talk if Derek was up for it. Or they could enjoy the silence.

Liam arrived before Derek. For a few moments, he was afraid Derek had decided to bail. Derek's lime green kayak bobbing across the sand was a welcome sight.

"Nice morning," Derek said. "It's going to be a hot one."

"It'll be cool beneath the trees."

Derek set his kayak at the edge of the water. "Let's get out there."

"Right behind you."

They pushed off and floated out into the lake. It was a nice change. Completely still water. The beach was still empty so there was no noise other than birds. The beach would soon be crowded with families trying to escape the heat. But right now, it was just them.

Slow, measured strokes. They weren't in a rush.

"Did you have a good week at work?" Liam asked.

"Same as usual. Except, a crazy bar brawl broke out on Friday night."

"Oh, my god. What happened?"

"No idea. One second everything was quiet, the next tables and drinks were crashing everywhere. Took three of us to hold down one of the guys."

"Police?"

"The lead singer of the band phoned 911 for us."

"Does that happen often? Bar fights?"

"Never. It's usually pretty quiet in there."

They drifted below some low-hanging cedar boughs. "I had an exciting week. One of our regular patients was diagnosed cancer free."

"Oh, wow. That's awesome."

"Makes you feel good. That someone made it through the poison we're pumping into their bodies and came out the other side better for it."

"I don't know how you do it."

"I care about people."

"I've gathered that about you."

Liam slowed. "I care about you."

Derek lay his paddle across the cockpit opening and stared straight ahead into the trees. "Please don't think I don't want you … I do. I'm just not ready."

"You'll let me know when you are?"

Derek looked over his shoulder at Liam. "You'll know."

That's the best he could ask for. Derek was willing to work toward an intimate relationship between them. He just needed to give him time.

"I'll race you to the end of the lake," Liam said.

"You're on." Derek dug in and took off. Liam was close behind him. In the end, Derek reached the shore first. They sat there laughing for a few moments while they caught their breath.

The trip back down the lake was quiet. They hauled their kayaks onto the beach and headed for the parking lot. They were both in board shorts, so there'd be no stripping down in front of each other this time. Besides, the parking lot was filled with cars and parents with their kids.

Liam accepted Derek's help lifting his kayak onto the carrying rack. Liam went to stand outside his driver's door. Derek leaned against the back passenger door.

"Do this again on Thursday?" Derek asked. "Elk Lake?"

"Same time?"

"Maybe 7. I have to work at 11:30."

"I'm scheduled but I'll switch my shift with someone."

Derek frowned. "Don't mess up your work schedule for me."

"You're worth it." Liam smiled.

For a second it looked like Derek was about to kiss him. He certainly had a fire in his eyes. Instead, Derek reached out and brushed his fingertips down Liam's arm, elbow to wrist.

"I had fun today," Derek said.

Liam was having trouble concentrating. The feel of Derek's skin on his had stirred up a whole range of emotions. His gut twisted as Derek lowered his hand.

"So did I," he managed. "Looking forward to Thursday."

"Yeah." Derek walked backward, not taking his eyes off Liam. "See you then." Then he turned and headed for his car, kayak in tow on his shoulder.

Liam slid into the driver's seat. He placed his forehead on the steering wheel as his heart tripped through all sorts of rhythms. Never—never had a man affected him like that.

Chapter Five | Derek

Derek nearly collapsed into the driver's seat of his car. His heart thundered in his ears. It had taken every bit of will he had not to kiss Liam. That need for contact had started with his hand.

He had needed to touch him.

It had been electrifying. Like Liam's skin was charged to react solely to his. He'd almost stepped in and closed his lips over Liam's mouth. To see if he could coax some sounds out of him.

This was going to be hard. Keeping his hands off him.

Then why are you doing it?

Derek pressed his eyes shut. He couldn't—he couldn't do it. Be intimate with a man. What would his friends think? How would it affect the rest of his life? Did he want to take that risk?

He gripped his steering wheel.

He wanted Liam.

When he imagined being with a man, it was purely sexual. The fact he and Liam were developing a friendship first was blindsiding him. Liam wasn't a faceless man in his fantasies. Liam was real. And he enjoyed hanging out with him. Craved his company.

Needed his touch.

Derek fired up his car and backed out of his spot. Out of the corner of his eye, he saw Liam's car still sitting in the parking lot. He drove slowly by it and looked in through the window.

Liam had his forehead on the steering wheel.

It affected him. Seeing Liam like that. Knowing Liam was struggling with the constraints they had placed on themselves. That he was suffering.

God dammit.

The impulse hit him. Derek threw open his car door and headed for Liam's car. Engine still running—driver's side door wide, he rapped hard on the glass of Liam's driver's side window.

It startled Liam. He jumped, then rolled down the infuriating barrier.

Derek reached in through the window, turned Liam's face, and at the most awkward of angles, pressed his lips to Liam's. His decision became clear as Liam raked his hand into Derek's hair.

He was willing to risk it all to be with this man.

Due to their positioning, they had to release each other much sooner than they would have liked. Plus, Derek's abandoned car was causing a traffic jam in the parking lot.

"Park your car," Liam whispered. "And come home with me."

"My kayak."

"We'll load it onto my rack."

Derek expected his brain to come up with a whole string of excuses not to do this, but his heart was overriding it. He couldn't think of a single reason not to go home with Liam.

His car parked, and kayak loaded, Derek slid into the passenger seat. Liam leaned across the center console and cupped Derek's face. The kiss he delivered was filled with profound passion.

He could've stayed like that. In that moment. Liam's

desire overtaking his very soul. As each kiss deepened in intention, Derek had no doubts he wanted to be somewhere else.

He pulled away. The look of concern on Liam's face was staggering. Liam thought he was changing his mind. Derek kissed him—softly. "Let's go," he whispered.

Liam threw the car into reverse and backed out of the spot. When they were on the road, Liam set his hand on Derek's thigh. Derek covered it with his and linked their fingers.

He knew Liam would take care of him.

Be gentle with him.

Be patient.

As they pulled up outside Liam's apartment, Derek's stomach fluttered. This was a huge step for him. Going back to a guy's place—with the intention of sex.

It was a world Derek had never thought he would ever enter. To be intimate with a man. He'd dreamed of it but had kept his desire locked down. Liam had ripped that deadbolt off.

They had trouble fitting both kayaks into the storage room but they managed. There was no elevator in Liam's building so they trudged up the stairs to the second floor.

Liam's apartment was eclectic. It suited the exposed brick walls that surrounded much of the space. He had large pictures of James Dean and Marilyn Monroe covering one wall up to the high ceiling. Half-naked men down another. A couple of women. It was obvious Liam had a preference.

Liam walked Derek backward until Derek was against the wall in the front entry. He closed in on Derek's mouth. The heat between them ignited. Derek hooked his fingers under Liam's light cotton shirt and hauled it off over Liam's head then dove back onto his lips. Liam tossed Derek's head aside with his chin and sought out his neck. He concentrated on the skin below Derek's ear down to his collarbone—kissing, sucking—licking. Derek couldn't contain a low moan.

"I want you so bad," Liam whispered.

"Go slow."

"For you. I would do anything."

Those words. They awoke something inside Derek. A deep yearning. He knew Liam spoke the truth. That he would take this as slow as he wanted. That he would do that for him.

Liam pushed Derek's shirt up and bent forward to take one of Derek's nipples into his mouth. Tiny circles—sucking. Then the other. Derek ran his hands through Liam's hair. He tipped his head back, sinking into the euphoria. The attention was tender—caring.

Derek gasped as Liam set kiss after kiss down between his ribs to his stomach. His cock was aching for Liam to descend further. Liam's hands rounded Derek's hips to his ass as he sunk to his knees. Liam dug his fingers into the cheeks of Derek's ass as he kissed and mouthed Derek's cock through the fabric of his shorts. He hauled Derek forward to increase the contact.

Derek groaned, his heart thumping.

Liam released Derek's ass with one hand and moved it around to Derek's cock and massaged it—stroking and caressing it through his shorts until it was rock hard.

"You all right," Liam checked in.

Derek could barely form words. "God, yes."

He dug his hands into Liam's hair as Liam lowered Derek's shorts and sucked his cock into his mouth. Slow, longing surges and retreats, Liam's tongue and lips sought to drive him insane.

Liam's mouth—warm and wet, his hands caressing. One on his shaft, the other playing with his balls. Derek couldn't back away from the edge. He grunted, jerked, and came.

Liam keep him nearly swallowed the entire time. When his body calmed, Liam sucked him root to tip, then released him. Staying near the floor, Liam peeled Derek's shorts off his feet, rose, reached for Derek's hand, and led him down a hallway into a bedroom.

Standing at the side of the bed, Liam stripped off his shorts and climbed onto the mattress.

Derek's breath caught in his chest. Liam's body was as toned as he'd imagined it would be. His pecs pronounced. His abs cut. His cock … god, his cock. And muscular, powerful thighs.

"Come here." Liam held out his hand to Derek.

Derek removed his shirt, took hold of Liam's hand, and joined Liam on the bed. He was trembling. He had no idea what was going to happen next.

Liam brought Derek down for a kiss then rolled them both so Derek was beneath him. The weight was different than Derek was used to. As was the incredible feeling of Liam's hard cock prodding him. Liam was all man. He met the next kiss with that carnal knowledge.

Liam groaned as their tongues danced between their lips.

Whatever Liam had planned next—Derek didn't care.

He trusted him.

The undulation of Liam's hips had Derek's cock waking

up. Thrust and retreat against his stomach. Liam's mouth on his. Liam's arms to either side of him. Derek wrapped his legs around Liam's thighs and rode the waves of Liam building to climax.

When Liam came, Derek felt the warmth on his belly. Then the slickness as Liam's cock slid back and forth through it. Derek's cock thickened. He held Liam's face and kissed him.

He could do this all over again and not be satisfied.

Liam dropped onto the bed beside him. The loss of the feel of Liam's body on top of him had Derek reaching for the man. Their lips met with a new understanding of each other.

"You doing okay?" Liam asked

"More than okay."

"In that case …."

Derek shivered as Liam brushed his fingers down his body and encased his cock. It was slowly recovering. Liam shuffled down the bed and took it into his mouth.

Derek placed both his hands on Liam's head and guided him.

He wouldn't be getting his car until much later in the day.

On and off for four hours. Derek had never experienced anything like it. The caring attention. The gentleness. The infuriating teasing. Derek was now addicted to Liam's mouth.

They'd napped. They'd snacked. They'd filled up on orange juice. Then they'd found each other beneath the sheets. Entwined, thrusting, kissing—cumming.

Two showers. One to get dirty. One to get clean. They'd

eventually removed the upper bedding from the bed. The mattress had turned into their nest for the duration of their day together.

Derek had trouble tearing himself away. But he was working at 6:30. Liam drove him back out to Thetis Lake to retrieve his car. They shared a long, desperate kiss in the parking and Derek made a promise to phone Liam when he finished work, no matter how late it was.

His joy must have been showing.

"Wow," Richard said as he waited for his drink order. "Never seen you look so happy." He tapped the bar mat. "Let me guess … you had sex with Liam."

Derek scowled at Richard. "Shh. I don't want anyone to know about us."

"He's not going to like that."

"What do you mean?"

"He's not into hiding his relationships in public. You need to prepare yourself for that if you're going to keep seeing him. Everyone is going to know."

It hit him like a rock to the head. Derek felt like he was going to be sick. Ramped up with lust, he'd tossed off his concerns, but now, back at work—his decision changed.

No one, aside from Richard, could ever find out about this.

Derek dried a dozen glasses at a furious pace. He needed to fix this. Tell Liam he wasn't interested in continuing. That the sex had been fun but he had no intention of doing it again.

He was determined to follow that path until Liam walked into the bar.

As Liam approached the bar stools, Derek couldn't take

his eyes off him. His heart tripped through an incredible series of rhythms. His chest heaved. There was no way he was going to give up dating that man. Seeing Liam again—it felt like coming home.

"What are you doing here?" Derek asked.

"Decided I needed a drink after a very exhausting day." Liam winked at Derek, then extended his hand across the bar. Derek could feel the flush creep up his neck. What was Liam expecting him to do? Take his hand? Liam knew he wasn't ready for this.

It was so tempting, though. Just to touch him again. To feel that spark. Derek checked around him to make sure no one was watching, then gave Liam's hand a quick squeeze.

That seemed to satisfy Liam.

"Small steps," Liam said. "That's all I ask."

"That's a big ask." Derek ripped a chit off the machine and grabbed a couple of glasses and pulled the first of two pints. "Especially when I'm at work."

"Is it, though? Anyone could have seen us kissing up Trounce Alley. Anyone could have seen us kissing in the Thetis Lake parking lot. You'll find most people don't care."

Derek set the glasses on the bar mat. "So what is this we're doing that people aren't going to care about? Because I can tell you … my friends will care."

"We're just dating."

Just dating?

Then how come it felt like more than dating? It felt like they were building something. Today, in Liam's bed, had been more than simple fun. There were thick ropes of bonds forming.

Regardless.

"I won't be introducing you to my friends any time soon," Derek said.

"Fine. I can wait."

"You're willing to do that for me."

"Like I said earlier today. For you—anything."

"And you meant that."

"Of course, I did. Anything you need." Liam moaned softly. "You make my entire body warm."

Derek leaned on the bar top. "I want to kiss you so bad right now."

"You'll have to hold that thought until later."

"When? When can I see you again?"

"Kayaking or rolling around in my sheets?"

"Either … both."

"I have Thursday off now. We can hit Elk Lake as we planned."

"Sounds great. I'm not working Thursday. I won't have to run off."

Liam smiled. "Perfect." He licked his lips. "I wasn't planning on actually having a drink, but I think I will, so I can watch you work. Now that I know what you look like beneath those clothes, intimately, I can content myself with watching you and picturing what lies under it all."

Derek cleared his throat as one of the servers stepped up to the bar to retrieve the pints. When she was gone, Derek shifted his weight and placed both hands on the bar.

"If you're trying to make me hard at work, you're going to succeed if you keep it up."

"Then I better stop." Liam tapped the bar top. "Gin and tonic."

Chapter Six | Liam

Wednesday dragged on. Liam was only four hours into his shift and he was getting restless. His mind wasn't on his work as much as it should be. Every once in a while, Derek's nude body, writhing in his bed, would infiltrate his thoughts. He only needed to hold out for one more day.

"You're off in la-la land again." One of the nurses, Karen, bumped him with her elbow.

"Sorry. Seeing someone new. He's on my mind."

Karen closed the papers on her clipboard. "Can I make an observation?"

"Sure."

"You only get like this when you're dating men."

Liam shrugged. "I prefer them … no secret."

"And this new guy, what's he like?"

"Broody but under it all there's a light about him. He's almost innocent."

"A project?"

"Not really. He'll get there on his own with a little attention."

"You see this one lasting?"

That was a loaded question. His brain was saying no. His heart was saying yes. He was going to take each day as it came. Not fight it—not push it.

"I don't know. Maybe."

"*Maybe* if you finally settled down, you could keep your mind on your work."

"Noted." Liam headed for the pharmacy to pick up the

medication that was ready for one of his patients. *Settle down*. He couldn't imagine that being in his future. He didn't trust anyone to stick around long-term. His life had been full of upheaval. No one stayed by his side.

Liam had attempted it once. Opened himself up to love. One year in and Brian had decided he wanted to take a job in Ontario. The timing had sucked. Liam had recently connected with his brother for the first time. They'd grown up apart from each other. Having his big brother in his life after so many years was something he couldn't walk away from. Brian had left without him.

He'd doubled down on guarding his heart after that.

Liam hung the bag of chemotherapy drugs. "Let's get you started." He programmed the machine attached to the IV pole and ensured it was dripping properly. This patient was new. A young woman—breast cancer. Barely nineteen. It was indiscriminate, cancer.

"Can I have another warm blanket?" she asked.

"Absolutely."

He headed back across the room toward the blanket warmer. Derek gasping and sighing as he came filled his mind. He couldn't get enough of him. Forever in bed would be too little.

He pulled a blanket from the machine and brought it to his patient. He unfolded it and laid it across her lap, making sure her feet were covered. "Better?"

"That's wonderful. Thank you."

"Did you take your anti-nausea pills?"

"Yes." She looked at her hands. Her name was Deanna. Liam touched her thigh. "If you need anything or have any questions, you flag me down, all right?"

Deanna reached out and grabbed his sleeve. "I'm scared."

Liam took a second and pulled up a chair. "This will give you a real chance to beat this."

"What if it doesn't work?"

"Then you'll know you tried everything you could to survive. I've heard that brings some people some peace." Liam leaned forward. "Do you have family?"

"My mom is on her way. Flies in tomorrow to be here for me."

"That'll be some comfort and give you a chance to rest. You'll need to rest."

"I'm sure my mom will be all over that. Cooking—cleaning. Taking the dog out."

"Sounds like you'll be set." Liam rose to his feet. "Take one day at a time." That's the advice he was giving to himself. Spend time with Derek—enjoy him. See where it took them.

"Thank you." Deanna smiled at him. "I appreciate you taking the time."

"It's my honor to be here for you."

Liam rechecked her drip, then headed for his next patient. Warren. Bladder cancer. He was palliative but they were trying immunotherapy on him anyway. There was always a chance.

Elk Lake was gorgeous to paddle on. It was a big lake. The perimeter of it and Beaver Lake was 10km. It would take 2.5 hours to paddle around the perimeter.

"Hey, Derek ... slow ... look." Liam pointed into the trees. At the very top of an immense cedar, a bald eagle was perched. They were privileged with witnessing it swoop down and scoop a fish out of the water, then return to its roost.

"Holy," Derek exclaimed. "That was awesome."

"I know what else is awesome."

Liam paddled up alongside Derek. He reached for the edge of Derek's cockpit and brought his kayak tight against Derek's. Derek figured out what he wanted. Liam, with extreme caution, leaned far enough to meet Derek in the middle for a swift kiss.

"Yum." Liam pushed away. "That'll hold me until we're back in the car."

Their morning on the lake ended in time for lunch. They picked a pub halfway back into town. It had originally been a carriage stop. It was quaint and incredibly old. They were seated in an area that might have been the stables. It was hard to tell after years of renovations.

Liam smirked.

He'd barely made it back to the car once they pulled their kayaks out of the water. He had been hot, hard, and yearning for attention. Derek had covertly jacked him off in the car.

"I'm going to try their wings," Liam said.

"Me too. Hot. You?"

"Not into the hot stuff. Blue Moon is more my style. Love me some blue cheese."

Derek made a face. Obviously, not a fan.

"Are you into sports?" Derek asked.

"Not really. Maybe a bit of soccer."

"I played some football on a men's weekend team about a decade ago."

"Wow … okay. That's really hot." Liam moved his foot

so it was between Derek's. He stroked his toe up and down Derek's calf. "You're certainly built like a tight end."

Derek laughed softly.

Every once in a while a small spark would light up the corner of Derek's eyes. Usually when Liam was teasing him. And when Derek came, the glimmer was enhanced. There had to be a way to keep him there. Build from there. Something was stopping Derek. He'd love to know what.

"So you were teased in school," Liam said after they ordered their food.

"Relentlessly. Being poor … having no parents."

"Kids teased you about that?" His own experience at school was something he'd prefer to forget. Being moved from school to school all his young life had left a mark. Being the new kid all the time and knowing any new friends he made were going to be ripped away from him soon enough because he'd get passed along—he didn't trust the universe.

"I used to get beat up," Liam said.

Derek reached across the table for him. "You and me both."

Liam slipped his hand into Derek's. It was the first time Derek had taken the initiative in public. It felt good. He ignored the stares. He'd lied to Derek. People did care about two men showing affection for each other. He caught Derek glancing around at the people watching them, but to his credit, he didn't let go. In fact, he squeezed Liam's hand harder.

"Kids are cruel," Liam said.

"We don't have to worry about them anymore. Or anyone else for that matter."

Liam steadied his breathing. Derek was sending a clear message. He was considering moving out of the shadows. He wanted to shout and share, but he'd let Derek do it at his speed. For the first time in his life, he felt like he had all the time in the world to explore with someone.

"I'm not worried when I'm with you," Liam said.

Derek released Liam and leaned back as the wings were placed in front of them.

"You sure you don't want to try a hot one?"

"Absolutely not."

Derek lifted the first wing to his mouth. By the time he hit his fourth one, his face had turned beet red. Liam felt obliged to tease him about it. When Derek started sweating, Liam couldn't contain himself. The suggestion of a shower when they got back to Liam's place picked up the speed by which the wings were being devoured. They were soon out of there.

Liam curled into Derek's embrace, skin against skin. He felt safe there. Like the world wouldn't be tugged out from under him while he slept. He closed his eyes. Even the sound of Derek's sleeping breaths calmed him. And the scent of him—it was soothing.

He was confident where his heart was sitting.

He was in the danger zone.

"You can't sleep?" Derek mumbled.

"A lot on my mind."

"Anything you want to share."

Liam squirmed tighter into Derek's arms. "Seeing my brother tomorrow."

"And you're worried about that?"

"It's mostly all right to see him. It's when he starts filling me in on what my mom is up to that things get uncomfortable."

"He goes to see her?"

"He goes and *finds* her."

Derek lifted his head. "What do you mean?"

"She's homeless. Lives in a tent downtown across from the shelter."

"God." Derek lowered his head. "That has to be damned stressful for you."

"She's been out there for years. She copes."

"She still uses drugs?"

"Yeah. It's a miracle she's alive," Liam replied.

"So … you have a brother."

"Yeah. Older than me. We didn't grow up together."

"Different foster homes?"

Liam tensed up.

Derek felt it because he rose on one elbow so he could see Liam's face.

"What happened?" Derek asked.

Liam had never told anyone this. He'd never trusted anyone enough to share such a painful part of his life. Derek was different. His feelings for the man were intense. He trusted him.

"My mom kept him. Kept him … got rid of me."

"Jeezus." Derek cupped Liam's face. "That's not your fault."

"Sure feels like it. Getting bounced from home to home my whole young life because I was a problem sure felt like it was my fault."

"They're idiots. Those people had no idea what they were

missing out on."

"You don't believe that."

Derek scowled at him. "I bloody well do." He closed the gap to Liam's lips and kissed him. He gazed down at him. "What do I have to do to prove it to you?"

Tears rolled down Liam's cheeks.

"Liam, please." Derek wiped some tears off Liam's cheeks.

There was only one thing Liam wanted from Derek. "Make love to me. Properly. None of this rubbing off on each other we've been doing. I need to feel you inside me."

Derek's hesitation had Liam gasping for breath. He needed this from Derek. He needed to feel wanted—worthy. He needed to feel cherished—loved. Even if it wasn't real, he needed it.

Derek brushed his fingers across Liam's lips. "I want everything with you."

Liam ran his hand into Derek's hair and pulled him to his mouth. Derek would have no idea what he was doing. But he'd get him there. Then pure loving bliss would follow.

"Bedside table," Liam whispered against Derek's lips once they parted. "Condoms and lube. Bring them here. I'll show you what to do."

Derek scurried off, then was back. He had the first part down with no problem. He ripped open a packet and rolled a condom onto his hardening cock.

Liam made himself comfortable on his back. He spread his legs and lifted his balls out of the way. He grabbed the lube and squirted a dollop down his crack.

"Watch," he said.

He closed his eyes and sunk his forefinger into his hole.

Back and forth—in and out. Two fingers. Then three. He opened his eyes and looked at Derek. "Your turn. Get some more lube."

Derek coated his fingers and shuffled in between Liam's legs. Liam groaned. Derek's fingers were thick and he had started with two. By the time he added a third, Liam was writhing.

Liam tapped Derek's hand to stop him and reached for him.

"Come here. I need you."

Derek hovered above him, then lowered himself to kiss Liam. As the heat between them became too much, Derek sat back on his heels. He filled his palm with lube and stroked his cock, coating it. Back above Liam, he appeared to be taking a moment.

"I want you to know something," Derek said. "We've only known each other a short while, but I feel like we've bonded." Derek brushed his fingers down Liam's cheek as he gazed down at him. "It wouldn't be premature of me to say I adore you."

Liam's heart skipped and jumped.

Dammit.

He reached for Derek and brought him down to his mouth. He wanted to swallow him whole. Have him become a part of his being. Part of his soul. Occupy every single piece of him.

Fumbling fingers, then Derek figured it out. The head of Derek's cock breached Liam's ring of flesh. Inch by inch, Liam took him in. The tears were flowing hard by the time Derek's hips closed in against his thighs. He'd never believed anyone before, but he knew Derek wasn't lying.

This incredible man felt him worthy of adoration.

Thrust—and retreat, spiraling him higher. Slow and easy. Loving. Liam wrapped his arms around Derek and dug his fingers into his shoulders.

As Derek kissed his collarbone, he came hard, convulsing and whispering. Every pulse rocked Liam's psyche. The emotions—goddamned, the emotions. His world was being flung into orbit.

He wasn't sure he'd ever recover.

Derek kissed Liam's breastbone as he slid from his ass. Liam applied pressure to the top of Derek's head as Derek descended. And for the first time, he felt the warmth of Derek's mouth around his cock. He closed his eyes and groaned. Derek's mouth was made for sucking cock. He paid attention. With every groan and undulation of Liam's hips, Derek made note and repeated what he had been doing. It wasn't long until Liam spilled down Derek's throat.

Derek crawled back up Liam's body, grinning.

There—right there. Some light in his eyes.

Liam welcomed Derek's lips on his. They rolled onto their sides, kissing as they kept a firm grip on each other's faces. Their pace was leisurely. They had all the time they'd ever need.

Liam breathed in a short breath.

He had something important he wanted to say. It had been on his mind. Derek's admission of adoration and their most recent lovemaking solidified his desire to move forward.

"I don't want to date anyone else," he said.

"I decided that ages ago."

"So … what does that mean to you?"

Derek exhaled across Liam's lips. "That we're a couple."

"And you're ready for that?"

"I'm ready for anything. I adore you."

Liam smiled and kissed Derek. He'd never get tired of hearing that. Derek spoke it from his heart. Joy didn't come easily to Derek. But it was in his eyes when he said those words.

Liam adjusted the collar on his shirt and knocked on the door of his brother's house. The house was opulent. Grand with impeccable landscaping. His brother was a successful criminal lawyer.

The door popped open and a face halfway down the doorjamb looked up at him.

"Unca Liam!"

"Hey, kiddo." Liam tossed the hair on Cameron's head. He was five going on fifteen. He was obstinate and thought he knew everything. "Can I come in?"

Cameron stepped back. "We having dinner wiff you."

"That's right." Liam wasn't sure what else to say. He was terrible with kids. Even two years of knowing Cameron hadn't made him better at it.

"Hey, Liam." His brother Lucas reached out for Liam's hand and shook it. They still weren't at the hugging stage. He only saw his brother once a month for dinner or coffee. They were still getting to know each other. At least some parts of their lives. He still wasn't *out* to his brother.

It went against his *out-and-proud* policy, but this was different. This was his brother. He didn't want to risk losing him after his brother had tracked him down. It was a big enough city that it was unlikely he would run into Lucas.

Especially since Liam tended to be out with his male dates at night. His brother never headed downtown for anything other than his office and the provincial courthouse. And that was during the day. He lived in Metchosin. He felt like his brother lived too far away to be having nights out downtown. So far, he'd been right.

"How's work?" Lucas led him into the living room.

"Unfortunately, busy. I wish I had nothing to do every day."

"Wouldn't that be something? A cure."

"I hold out hope for one."

"Hey, Liam." Rebecca walked into the living room. "Drink?"

"Do you have a cider?"

"That we do. Glass?"

"Yes, thanks ... a glass." Liam sunk onto a seat of the long sofa dominating the space. Lucas sat across from him. "So, how's your work going?" Liam asked.

"Same old. Not much of anything exciting."

"Well, I suppose that's good."

"Might have a murder trial coming up."

"Oh ... nice."

It made him uncomfortable that his brother defended the accused. Especially, serious crime. He would have preferred if Lucas were a tax lawyer or something.

"Saw Mom," Lucas said.

Liam nearly cringed. He didn't like that word, *Mom*. She'd never been a mom to him. She'd barely been a mom to Lucas. His brother had told him horror stories about her missing for days. And him having to fend for himself as early as the age of seven. How he'd been tormented because of his dirty clothes and bad hygiene and lack of a proper lunch. When he'd turned nine, he'd figured out he could use his mom's credit card to buy food. He just needed to tap it. That only lasted so long because their mother didn't pay the credit card bill. Lucas had taken to begging for money.

"Yeah, how's she doing?"

"Had to buy her another tent. Says the last one was stolen."

Liam tensed. He knew damn well she had probably sold the tent and everything in it for drug money. His brother, for some reason, thought he could *save* their mother. It hadn't worked so far and it had been fifteen years since Lucas started the quest.

"I have her booked into a treatment center," Lucas said. "She goes in next week."

Yup, then she leaves a week later. His mother had gone into nine treatment centers now under Lucas' watchful eye. Liam had given up trying to tell his brother he was wasting his money.

"Hopefully, it sticks this time," Liam replied.

"Me too." Lucas took a sip of his drink. "Rebecca tells me you're seeing someone."

Liam smiled. "I am. And they're amazing."

"Name?"

"I'm not telling. They're a bit shy about people knowing about us."

Lucas scowled. "Weird. Why?"

Liam shrugged. "Not sure. Not going to fight it, though." He took the glass Rebecca offered him. He had intended to tell his brother. To *come out* to him. But the thought of potentially losing Lucas from his life after they'd been apart for so long terrified him.

He wasn't ready to risk it.

He wanted to tell Lucas about Derek. How the man was bringing him so much joy. That they had a companionship that was intense and profound. That he had developed feelings for him.

He wanted to tell him all those things. To share the happiness overflowing in his life.

But he couldn't. He couldn't do it.

In a matter of time, it would all come to a crashing end anyway.

An uncomfortable urge coursed through his body. It was a familiar one. One that would tear everything apart he had built with Derek. His mind had been shouting at him to run.

It took every ounce of his will to fight his impulse.

Chapter Seven | Derek

The tent was a bit of a menace. Liam had warned him it required a lot of patience. This was insane, though. "Are you sure we have all the poles in the right places this time?"

"Should be good to go."

They bent the poles and slipped the feet into the pockets of all six corners. This time, the damned thing looked like a proper tent. Liam pounded the tent pegs into the ground to secure it as best he could. The area they were camping in was practically one big rock.

They weren't expecting rain. The weather had been cooling but it was a lovely September. They wouldn't need the rainfly. Instead, they could enjoy glimpses of the trees above them.

Derek arranged the double sleeping bag they had picked up in the tent. Single sleeping bags were not going to do the trick. They were going to take full advantage of the solitude.

They had paddled to the small, secluded island they'd explored together months back to spend some time together without any interruptions of daily life.

Liam wrapped Derek up in his arms and kissed him.

He held Derek out at arm's length. "Isn't this great?"

Derek huffed a laugh. "Yet to be determined."

"I can't believe you've never been camping."

"My grandparents had enough trouble keeping me contained without setting me loose in the woods. They wouldn't have had the energy to rein me in."

"Your grandparents. Are they both gone?"

"Yeah. Grandad recently. He was eighty. We lost Grandma two years ago."

"I'm sorry."

Derek shrugged. "He was the last of my family. Both my mom and dad didn't have any siblings. I'm sure there are people out there related to me, but no one close. It's just me."

"No, it's not. You're not alone." Liam reached for Derek's hand. That was a big statement for Liam. Monumental for someone who was skittish about long-term relationships.

It gave Derek a sliver of hope. Potentially *coming out* for someone who might be gone in a few months … made him nervous. He still wasn't sure he could do it.

Derek smiled. "I don't feel alone when I'm with you." He could feel Liam tense like he wanted to take back his comment about Derek not being alone.

Liam spun and headed for a ring of rocks. "I'm glad we had most of that wood split before we hauled it out here. Didn't want to be carting along an axe as well."

"You're sure you can start a fire."

"Better hope so, or it's going to be a little cold."

Derek set his hands on Liam's shoulders and massaged them. "I'll keep you warm."

"Maybe so, but I also want a hot dinner."

"Can't help you there." Derek wasn't looking forward to the dehydrated meals Liam had insisted on bringing. Apparently, the lasagna was palatable. He would've preferred a can of beans.

Liam poured some of the water they had brought into a kettle, then set about getting the fire started. After a few false starts, Liam had the beginnings of something promising. As they added wood, the fire grew. It was giving out a decent amount of heat in no time.

"Okay, just need to boil this water," Liam said. "Can you grab the lasagna packets?"

Derek went into the tent and dug around in Liam's backpack until he found them. He stuffed everything else back into the pack. He smiled. There were a hell of a lot of condoms in there.

He brought the vacuum-sealed packets back to the fire. He motioned for Liam's jackknife and used it to open the foil. The packets expanded. He looked in one. Everything looked desiccated.

"Look up at the sky," Liam said.

The sky was lit up with pink and blue streaks as the sun set. It was beautiful. The display of nature and the smell of campfire stirred something primal in him. Derek wandered up behind Liam and wrapped his arms around him. He kissed the back of Liam's neck.

"This *was* a good idea," he said.

"I'm full of good ideas."

"Jury is still out on the food."

"You have to trust me."

"You have no idea how much I trust you," Derek said as he hugged Liam tighter. "And how much I want to be with you, but I'm not sure I'm ready to tell everyone."

"Still worried about introducing me to your friends?"

"Terrified."

"And work?"

"You come in so much when I'm working and sit at the bar, watching me, I think most of them have figured it out."

"Or they think I'm some kind of stalker."

Derek laughed and kissed the back of Liam's head. "A gorgeous one I have no intention of getting rid of."

Liam turned in Derek's arms. "I think the water is boiling. It's spitting all over the logs."

Derek rolled his eyes. "I guess it's time to force this food down."

"So many other things I'd rather force into your mouth."

Derek snorted. "Later."

Liam held the packets open as Derek poured the water into them. They let them steep then dug in. Derek had to admit, they weren't too bad. Less food than he'd normally eat but Liam had brought a big bag of packets; different foods. He shouldn't starve to death in two days.

The fire was roaring by the time they finished eating. The sun down and darkness upon them; the only light, the flickering flames. It was cozy and relaxing to sit there looking into the fire.

"Marshmallows," Liam said and struggled to his feet. He brought back a bag of marshmallows and two sticks he'd been whittling earlier. He handed one to Derek.

I've never done this before."

"Follow my lead." Liam speared two marshmallows on his stick and held it just above the flames. "The trick is to not set them on fire. Unless you like them black and crispy."

"Do I turn it?"

"Yeah, you want to get all sides brown."

After a few minutes, Derek's marshmallows started to droop off the stick.

"They're done," Liam said. "Take them off quick."

Derek moved the stick away from the flames and used

his fingers to pull off the marshmallows and deposit them in his mouth. His fingers were a mess by the time he finished.

"Put those inner bits back over the fire," Liam said.

"My fingers are all sticky." Derek abandoned his roasting stick.

Liam smiled and dropped the second roasting of his marshmallows into the fire. "Let me help you with that." He took Derek's hand and brought it to his mouth. One finger after another, he sucked and licked Derek's skin until it was clean. Derek's cock pressed hard against his jeans. He shifted on the log they were sitting on. "Undo your pants," Liam said.

Derek looked around, not actually expecting to see anyone. They had checked. There was no one else on the island tonight. He undid his button and fly and released his cock from its confines.

Liam kneeled in the dirt and took Derek's cockhead and shaft into his mouth. He ran his tongue up and down its length; his lips applying the perfect pressure.

Liam backed off and spit on it, pumped it a few times with his hand, then dove back on. Too many more rounds of that and Derek was going to cum. Liam sucked him to the tip, then ran off toward the tent. Circles of light from the flashlight Liam had taken with him illuminated the tent.

He walked back across the campsite and handed Derek a condom and packet of lube.

"Out here?" Derek had been expecting they would be having sex in the tent. Not out here. Not in the open. *There's no one here*. A coil of lust curled around in his gut, accompanied by a wave of fervent impatience, and he was quick to get Liam's pants around his ankles and sort out the supplies Liam had given him. A gust of air made the fire crackle.

Liam kneeled in front of him, his body aglow with an orange hue from the flames. Derek kneeled behind him. With one hand he grabbed Liam's hip and pressed into Liam—slow. Once he was closed in against his ass, he stroked his other hand down Liam's back, neck to tailbone.

He adored this man.

Derek lingered on his skin.

God ... it was so much more than that.

They'd spent the past month sharing so much about themselves. Hopes. Dreams. Regrets in life. Passions. They often spent hours on the phone at night when they weren't together.

Derek adjusted his knees. The ground was rocky and hard. He just needed to find the right spot. He retreated from Liam's hole, then slid back in—gently.

Each stroke was measured and loving. He changed the position of his hands. He grabbed Liam's shoulders to keep him from moving and thrust a little faster.

The sounds. The sounds Liam made. They had always been conscious of the neighbors while in their apartments. Out here, though. Liam could be as loud as he wanted.

And he wanted to be loud.

Derek joined him. Grunting and swearing until he came—hard. He reached around and encased Liam's cock, pumping it until Liam spilled onto the rocky ground.

They rode through Liam's every jerk and pulse, then Derek leaned forward and kissed Liam's back, and withdrew his cock. He wasn't entirely satisfied. He preferred to see

Liam's face when he came. To watch his eyelashes flutter, his back arch—his mouth open, longing to be kissed.

They had all weekend.

He'd be making love to Liam every chance he got. He'd never felt as well matched sexually with anyone in his life. They moved together in sync like they'd been designed to do so.

Liam jumped up and pulled his pants into place.

"I love doing it outdoors," Liam said.

Doing it.

Such an insufficient word for what they had together.

Derek got up off his knees. "Later in the tent, I'm going to worship every bit of you."

"Mmm." Liam wandered up to him and put his arms around Derek's neck. "I'm up for that … as long as I can do it back."

Derek took the opportunity to kiss Liam. His lips were the most responsive Derek had ever encountered. They always wanted more—deeper—longer. Their tongues mingled.

When they pulled away, they were both breathing heavily.

"Tent," Liam suggested. "We can rest a bit … then build it slow."

"What about the fire?"

Liam pulled away. "We'll have to put it out." He dumped the kettle on the fire, then handed it to Derek. "Go down to the ocean. Fill it up. I'll start stirring the embers."

Derek skidded down to the ocean with a flashlight, filled the kettle, then scrambled back up the incline. He had to do it two more times before the fire finally relented and went out.

"Now—tent," Derek said and Liam followed him.

Even though it was a bit chilly, they stripped off their clothes and tucked up together inside the sleeping bag. They sought each other out for warmth. Liam curled into Derek's embrace.

Derek loved falling asleep and waking up with Liam at his side. It was meant to be. He could feel it in his heart. Liam hadn't expressed any emotions to indicate he was feeling the same way. He acted like he was. They often spent strings of days together. At no point did Derek ever feel like he'd had enough and wanted away from Liam. And at no point had it ever seemed like Liam wanted to kick him out for a few days. Derek could carry on like that forever— together.

"Roll over," he whispered to Liam. "Move up a bit."

Derek tossed the sleeping bag aside so he'd have more room. They would just have to withstand the cold air. It added to the sensations coursing through his body.

He set a line of kisses down Liam's spine to his tailbone. He adjusted his body to be between Liam's legs. With his hands, he spread Liam's ass checks. He used his thumb to caress Liam's hole then tipped forward and licked it. It felt tight and rigid. It was one of his favorite spots to be.

He circled and prodded it with his tongue. Liam squirmed, sighing and moaning as he helped to hold one cheek aside. Derek used his thumbs to pry it open and spit at it. He massaged the fluid into Liam's hole, then attacked the relaxing hole with his mouth.

Derek came up for air. "Roll back over."

Liam rolled and scooted until Derek was back between

his legs. Derek pressed Liam's hard cock against his belly and lifted one of his balls into his mouth. He rotated his tongue around it—wetting—caressing. Then dragged it down as he freed it from his mouth. He went after the other. Giving it the same treatment. Liam's cock came next.

By the time he was finished, Liam was writhing and undulating his hips, and grasping handfuls of Derek's hair. Panting—groaning. He gripped Derek's shoulder.

"Please … Derek. I want you."

Derek dug for another condom and lube packet. This time he was able to gaze into Liam's eyes. Stroke after stroke brought them closer together. There was a moment when Derek thought he saw something in Liam's eyes. A glimmer of the devotion he felt growing within his own soul.

It was there and then it was gone.

Liam was suppressing it. And Derek knew why. This was normally when Liam would cut and run. Liam was fighting it. Liam didn't want what they had together to end either.

After, when Derek held Liam, he kissed Liam's forehead.

"Talk to me," he said.

"About what?"

"About what's going through your head. About us."

Liam sighed. "What's to talk about?"

"I can feel you're holding back."

Liam stroked his fingers through the hair on Derek's chest. "I'm scared."

"Scared of what?"

"I'm scared I'm going to leave you."

Derek shifted. "Have you thought about it? That you want to leave?"

"It creeps up on me every single day."

Derek clung to Liam. He never wanted to let him go. He wouldn't stop Liam from leaving him but it would devastate him. He buried his face in Liam's hair.

"Please don't," he whispered.

"In my heart, I don't want to … but for some reason that triggers my brain into wanting to leave. I don't know why. If I pack down my feelings … maybe I can trick it."

"That's no way to live."

"Not sure what else to do."

"You're honestly afraid that if acknowledge your feelings, you'll want to run?"

"It's been my pattern."

"How far does that extend?" Derek asked.

"What do you mean?"

"We agreed we're a couple. Are you second-guessing that?"

"No. God, no. That's not what this is about."

"Okay. So, have you told your brother yet?"

Liam shook his head. "Haven't been able to do it. It makes it too real."

"It is real. What we have is real."

"Really what, though?" Liam turned in Derek's arms so he faced him. "What are we doing? Really? Do you see us together in five years?"

"I want that, but right now, I'm not seeing it. I don't know where I stand with you."

Liam closed his eyes. "Dammit, Derek."

"What?"

Liam opened his eyes and stared into Derek's. He touched Derek's face and shook his head. He was crying. "I can't stop it. I've tried … but I can't."

"Can't stop what? *Are* you going to leave me?"

"I don't want to. I'm fighting so hard …." Liam placed his forehead on Derek's. "I'm so in love with you, it fucking hurts. My mind is screaming at me to run."

Derek's heart jumped. He hadn't been expecting that at all. From zero to sixty in seconds. He hadn't thought it possible for Liam to fall in love. It went against his reputation.

The fact he had … Derek's soul filled to near bursting.

Liam had obviously been unsuccessful in packing down his feelings.

"And you've been trying to stop that? Your love for me?"

"I don't want it to end between us."

"Babe … god. It's not going to." Derek kissed Liam. "I love you too."

Liam turned his face away. "Now we've done it. Jinxed the whole damned thing."

"Why do you say that?"

"People move on without me, Derek. Always have … always will."

Derek turned Liam's head to face him. "I'm not going anywhere." Liam had to realize how deep down his love came from. From the base of his very essence. This man had experienced so little love in his life growing up, though … he wouldn't know what it looked like.

Chapter Eight | Liam

Liam was excited to introduce Derek to something different. He still couldn't believe Derek had never been to a drag show or seen any drag on television. He'd been sheltered from queer culture all his life. Hanging out with his heteronormative friends. Drag Brunch at one of the local gay bars downtown was going to be an eye-opener for him

"Did you withdraw the five-dollar bills I asked you to get?" Liam asked Derek. "Gotta make sure we have enough of them to tip the queens."

"Got a stack of them." Derek stayed close to Liam's side as they walked from the parking garage to the bar. Not quite holding hands … but close. Sometimes when they were walking together in public, they linked pinky fingers for brief moments. It never went beyond that. Liam was keeping his promise. They'd go as slow with the public displays as Derek wanted.

Their exchange of words of love continued and Derek checked in with him most days to see how Liam was doing in terms of their relationship. As time passed, Liam's urge to run subsided. The daily affirmations of love overwrote the entire impulse—almost.

They stepped inside the converted sushi restaurant. Green walls and cedar supports. Pride flags hung from post to post and there were pictures of drag performers decorating the walls.

"Reservation for Liam. 4." They were meeting some friends of Liam's. A male-male couple in their 60s. He hoped it would help Derek relax a little. Show him it wasn't a big deal to be in a same-sex relationship out in public. That it didn't have to be a big display.

Randy and Wes were the perfect people to do that. They'd been together so long, it was obvious they were a couple but they kept their public displays of affection to a minimum.

They were already there when Liam and Derek made their way to the table.

Liam was excited to introduce Derek.

"Hey, Liam," Both Randy and West said in unison.

"Guys." Liam grinned.

"And who do we have here?" Randy asked.

"This is the amazing man I was telling you about. Derek."

Randy reached for Derek's hand and shook it. "Nice to finally meet you, Derek. Liam has been going on about you for the last month. Goofy in love. Thought we were never going to meet the guy that seems to have pinned Liam down. No small feat, let me tell you."

"I've been told," Derek answered. He shook Wes's hand, then slid onto the bench seating beside Liam. Liam's body vibrated as Derek shoved him playfully with his shoulder.

Liam would have preferred more contact in public, but he was quick to hold tight to any little bits of affection Derek showed him.

"We've ordered a round of mimosas," Wes said. "Hope that's all right."

Liam flipped over a menu. "Fine by me." He perused the

options, then passed the menu to Derek. "Their bennies here are good."

"Is that what you're having?"

"Yeah, I like the smoked salmon one."

"You've been here a lot?"

"At least once a week. Until we started dating." Liam spun his water glass. "So glad you're here with me now. I kinda missed the place. Definitely missed seeing drag."

As if on cue, the show got underway. The host was a visiting queen from Kelowna, Trixie Lamour, and she was dressed in a silver sequined dress with ridiculously high shoes. Liam wasn't sure how Derek would react to the spectacle. He'd heard that Trixie had a smutty mouth on her. The sexual innuendoes started spilling out of her from the very first word. About herself. About any person she decided to interrogate. She worked the room—crass and hilarious.

Liam turned to look at Derek.

Oh, thank god.

Derek was laughing. Even clapping his hands on occasion along with everyone else. Liam had been worried Derek would hate it. Then a huge part of his life would be off the table. These were his people—this was his family. Giving them up would have left a massive hole in his heart.

The music started and Trixie Lamour launched into her lip-sync routine. She was animated and at times grotesque, but it was an adult-only bar, so the response was hooting and hollering, and whistles and cheers. Trixie sped around the space dancing, hanging off railings and beams—and people. Liam cracked up when Derek blew up clapping as Trixie did a death drop.

Liam leaned against Derek. When Trixie finished, Derek wrapped his arm around Liam's shoulders and kissed Liam on the cheek. Liam nearly floated away. It was the most affectionate Derek had been with him in public. He was thrilled Derek felt comfortable in this space.

"Derek?" A cute brunette woman approached the edge of their table. Derek was quick to whip his arm back away from Liam's shoulders.

"I thought that was you," she said.

Her face was pinched in confusion.

Dammit.

Liam knew exactly where this woman came from.

"Chelsea," Derek muttered.

Liam shuffled away from Derek, but it was already too late. This Chelsea woman had seen them getting cozy together.

"What are you doing here?" Derek asked.

"Out with some girlfriends. Thought brunch here might be fun." She furrowed her brow and pointed at Liam. "Who's this?"

Derek cleared his throat. "My friend, Liam."

Ouch.

That hurt.

Friend.

Chelsea put her hand on her hip. "Don't mess with me, Derek. What's going on?" It seemed this friend of Derek's wasn't about to let what she saw go and move on with her life.

Derek stroked his hand down his face. "Look, Chelsea … he's not actually my friend."

"Then who is he?"

Derek took and released a deep breath. He reached for Liam's hand and clung to it. Liam was there for him. He gripped Derek tight. "He's my boyfriend."

"I'm sorry … what?"

"My boyfriend, Chelsea."

"Boyfriend … as in you're seeing each other?"

"Yes."

"Like a couple?"

"Yes."

"Since when did you start dating men?"

"Liam is my first."

This baffled Chelsea. Her eyebrows pinched and she shook her head. "So what … you just woke up one day—gay?"

"Bisexual. And I've always been. It didn't just happen overnight."

"All those women I hooked you up with."

"Like I said—bisexual."

Derek was giving her way too much information. It was none of her damned business what his sexual identity was. Liam squeezed Derek's hand. His boyfriend had to handle this in his own way, though. If he wanted to spill, Liam wasn't going to stop him.

"And when did this start?" She waggled her finger back and forth between the two of them. "This *thing* between the two of you."

"We've been together for months. And it's more than a *thing*."

"More … what do you mean, more?"

Derek lifted their clasped hands. "We're in love."

Chelsea cupped her hand over her mouth. Her face was

flushed. "Oh, for fuck's sake, Derek. You've got to be kidding me."

"Not even a little bit."

"You can't be … you can't be gay. Jackson is going to freak the hell out."

"Not gay … and I don't care what Jackson thinks."

That was a step forward. Up until now, Derek had been especially worried about what his guy friends would think. If they'd accept him. If they'd still want to be his friend.

It seemed Derek was willing to risk those long-standing friendships for him. He slid back closer to Derek. They were together. Derek had said it aloud to one of his friends.

Chelsea shook her head. "I'm not telling Jackson. That's all on you." She looked toward the table she'd been sitting at. Her friends were watching the exchange. They looked concerned, probably wondering why their friend had approached a table of outwardly gay-looking men.

"I will," Derek said. "Soon."

Chelsea dipped her brow as she looked at him. "You're sure about this. With him."

It was more than Liam had been expecting, but Derek turned his face and planted a deep, passionate kiss on him. He kept his eyes locked on Liam afterward. "I love you."

"Love you too, babe."

When Liam looked back, Chelsea was gone. Back at the table with her friends. They were all leaning toward Chelsea, then shoulder-checking to look at Derek as Chelsea spoke.

Derek's secret was out. And in a big damned splashy way.

They were all over each other when they spilled through the door to Liam's apartment. Sharing an intense kiss and declaring their love for one another in a public space had fired them both up.

They'd left soon after the confrontation with Chelsea.

Derek slammed the front door and stripped the black, puffy coat off Liam. He dropped it on the floor and went after Liam's shirt. That soon joined the coat. Derek struggled out of his outerwear and shirt and added them to the pile of clothing in the front entry of the apartment.

They moved through into the living room; hands and lips seeking. Heaving breaths. Pants, underwear, and socks soon littered the carpet. Derek pushed Liam down on the sofa and layered his body on top of Liam's. Kiss after kiss—open mouths—tongues prodding.

Liam undulated his hips and pressed his cock to Derek's; grinding. He opened his legs and wrapped them around Derek. "Show me how much you love me."

Derek pulled away. His eyes were hooded with desire but also tinted with apprehension.

"Not tonight," he said. "Tonight, I want it to be me."

Liam blinked. As in what? Bottoming? It wasn't his preference to top, but he didn't think it would ever come up. Derek had never expressed any interest in trying it.

If that's what Derek wanted, though, he wasn't going to deny him.

He ran his fingers down Derek's cheek. "I want that with you."

Derek lifted himself off the sofa. "What do I do?"

"Let's stay here." Liam swung his legs off the sofa and sat. "Gives you more control." He pointed to a basket in the lower tier of the coffee table. "Grab the stuff."

Derek set the basket on the sofa. Liam ripped open a packet and rolled a condom into place.

"Come here," Liam said and patted his lap.

Derek climbed onto the cushions and straddled Liam's lap, facing him. Liam squirted some lube onto his fingers as Derek put his hands on Liam's shoulders to support himself. The look of love in Derek's eyes as he gazed down at him was breathtaking.

He loved this man with all his heart. Liam kissed Derek's chest as he reached around, found Derek's hole, and massaged it—gently.

Derek had no idea what he was in for.

When he was satisfied, he placed his hands on Derek's ass. Derek bent forward for a kiss and Liam used his fingers to guide his cock toward Derek's hole. He rubbed his cockhead around the ring he had worked to be as receptive as he could. He sunk in a short way.

"Fuck," Derek groaned.

"Relax, babe."

Derek closed his eyes and lowered himself ever so slowly. Liam moaned with each creeping inch. Derek's tight, velvety channel embraced his cock. He'd forgotten how good that felt.

Derek came to rest in his lap.

"You all right?" Liam asked.

Derek smiled. "Not sure yet." He cupped Liam's face and kissed him hard, then went back to using Liam's shoulders for support. He used his hips and thighs to rise, then dropped back.

Liam placed his hands on Derek's thighs, riding the up-

and-down motion. He kept his gaze on Derek's face. The moment pain turned to pleasure, wonderment scattered all over Derek's features.

"Jeezus," Derek whispered, then hovered above Liam's lips with his as he rose and sunk; ascending higher—faster, falling deep. He sat in Liam's lap and rotated his hips, grinding Liam's cock against the spot that was getting dragged across. Derek groaned, tossed his head back, and took his hand to his own cock. He licked his lips as he rode the sensation.

Liam took over for him, one hand on Derek's cock—the other pinching one of Derek's nipples. He switched to the other one as Derek's mouth fell open—a glorious sound escaping.

Wonderment—and lust—greed, and ecstasy.

The amount of stimulation had to be incredible.

Derek bounced in his lap—faster—harder; his cock hard in Liam's hand. The moment before Derek came, his ass clenched, clamping down on Liam's cock. Sublime spurts and droplets of cum soon decorated Liam's chest. He stroked his hand up Derek's chest and gripped his throat.

Liam received a groan in response. Derek gazed down at him.

He was fucking beautiful.

The light in Derek's eyes was almost complete.

Liam lowered his arm and grabbed tight to Derek's hips with both hands to hold him in place. He hammered up into Derek until he surged, grunted, and spilled into the condom.

He almost felt light-headed.

He massaged Derek's ass. Someday, he'd be able to spill directly into Derek—fill him. Have Derek fill him too. But that was a conversation that was still a ways off.

Derek gripped the back of the sofa and sunk onto Liam's mouth. When Derek pulled away, he was grinning. "I can see why you like that."

Liam brushed his hand across Derek's abs. "You would do it again?"

"Not often—but, yeah."

"Come back to me." Liam cupped Derek's face and drew him to his mouth. The kiss was slow—languid. He tried to pour his love into it. Derek had to know how desperate he was for him. Adoration and love and everything in between. His life was full with Derek by his side.

"I love you," Liam whispered against Derek's lips.

"You're my love eternal."

Liam pulled back. That was a big statement. It made that little part in his brain that wanted to run—squirm. Eternal was a bloody long time.

Derek's eyebrows dipped. "I'm sorry," he said. "I didn't mean to imply anything."

Liam closed his eyes and shook his head. "I have no right to contradict you. It's how you feel. I just don't know if I'm there yet."

"You don't need to be. Someone gave me good advice once. That we should enjoy each other. That's what I want to do." Derek lifted himself off Liam's cock. "See where it takes us."

"I can get behind that." Liam smiled. "I'm enjoying the hell out of you."

Every day with Derek was better than the last. The times they spent two and three days together were some of the best of his life. Derek was starting to feel like family. Like the family he never had. The essence of the family life he had dreamed of having.

"What are you thinking about?" Derek asked.

"I'm thinking that I really am hopelessly in love with you."

Derek sat beside him and gripped his hand. "That's a good place to start."

Chapter Nine | Derek

It came out of nowhere. One minute he was dreaming about him and Liam snowboarding—the next, he was hanging upside down in his toddler car seat.

Then the screaming started.

His mom crying and screaming, shouting at his dad to wake up. The smell of gasoline. His mom fell eerily silent. The creak and groan of the car filled the cabin. The straps of his car seat made his shoulders and hips hurt. His head was pounding. His heart even faster.

Mom?

Why had she stopped screaming?

Derek reached forward but couldn't reach her. He could hear her breathing.

Dad?

He'd been silent throughout the violent tumble.

Young Derek started to cry. Deep down he knew—he knew his dad was gone. Just like his sister Julie. She'd been silent like that. Days later, they'd lowered her body into the ground.

The car was illuminated by flashing lights.

His mom started screaming again. Lower in volume. Strained.

Terrified—and gurgling.

The front of the vehicle burst into flames.

Derek startled awake, sweating. His sudden jerking

motion woke Liam.

"What's going on? Another nightmare?" Liam asked.

Derek nodded. "Yeah."

"Your mom again?"

"Can't get that sound out of my head."

"I really think you need to see a therapist."

"You've said."

"You suffered an incredible trauma. It would mess with anyone's head."

Derek had finally told Liam about his nightmares. Night and after night, Derek would wake up thrashing around or crying out for his mom. After many nights of that, Liam figured out Derek had been in the car during the crash that killed his parents.

He still hadn't told Liam about his sister. He'd been so young, he had no memories of his big sister being well. They'd spent hours coloring together on her hospital bed. That he *could* remember. And when everything about her had stopped. He'd been holding her hand.

"I'll think about it," Derek replied.

Derek shuffled over until his back was pressed to Liam's chest. Ass to groin. His legs tangled with Liam's. He wanted all the contact with Liam he could get.

"Hold me," Derek said.

Liam slung his arm over Derek's body and kissed the base of his neck.

It's not enough.

Derek wanted more.

"Grab a condom," he whispered. It wasn't often but every once in a while, he needed Liam inside him, reminding him how much he was loved and cherished.

He shut his eyes as Liam pushed into him. Liam clung tight to him as he thrust—slow and gentle. Liam's rocking hips soothed him. Neither one of them even needed to cum. The joining of their bodies signified their commitment to one another. That they moved as one.

A tear trickled from Derek's eye.

He was ready. He was ready to risk it all and tell his friends about Liam.

His love for the man was absolute.

Derek kept telling himself it was just another night hanging out with the guys and watching a football game. Except, this time, he'd be bringing someone special along.

They were meeting at Darrell's house. Every one of his friends would be there.

Derek had told Jackson he was bringing someone for them to meet. He'd had a ton of questions but Derek had told him they'd answer everything during timeouts.

Chelsea had kept her promise—for months. After talking to Jackson, it was obvious Chelsea hadn't said a thing to Jackson about Liam.

They stood outside Darrell's door, the falling snow landing on their shoulders. It wasn't unreasonably cold but they'd been getting more snow than usual this winter.

Christmas was just over a week away.

"It might help if we knocked," Liam teased.

"Just gathering my nerve. They have no idea I'm into men."

"You might be surprised. I'm sure some of the other women have clocked you."

Derek rolled his shoulders, knocked on the door, swung

it open, and walked into the front entry. "Hey! We're here!" he shouted.

"Derek!"

Darlene, Jessie's girlfriend, bounced into the front entry from the living room. She came to an abrupt stop when she saw Liam standing beside him. "Who's this? I thought you were bringing your new girlfriend. Jackson said you had someone for us to meet."

She frowned. "Now, I'm disappointed."

Derek cleared his throat. "This *is* who I want you to meet." He brushed his knuckles against Liam's. He needed to touch Liam to calm his nerves. "This is Liam—my boyfriend."

Darlene squealed. She leaped forward and clung to Derek's biceps. "Why didn't you tell me? There are so many men at work I could've hooked you up with."

"You would do what?" Jackson wandered into the entry with them.

Darlene turned and touched Liam's chest. "This is— Derek's boyfriend."

Jackson scowled. "His what?"

Derek had expected a stand-off with Jackson. He wasn't the most liberal guy.

"My boyfriend. His name is Liam."

"I don't care what his bloody name is!" Jackson shouted. "Get him the fuck out of here!"

"What the hell is going on out here?" Darrell pushed Jackson out of the way.

"Him." Jackson pointed at Derek. "He brought a goddamned *boyfriend* with him."

Darrell shoved Jackson. "And you're surprised? Where

the hell have you been?" He reached out his hand to Liam. "Hey, I'm Darrell. Welcome."

"Thanks." Liam shook Darrell's hand and shook it. "Liam."

"Oh, no." Jackson shook his head. "We are *not* going to pretend this is okay."

Darrell's wife Tiffany leaned against the door frame. "Get over yourself, Jackson. Derek has been giving off man-loving vibes since the first day we met him."

Derek reached for Liam's hand, properly this time. He clung to Liam like he was the only thing keeping his kayak afloat in a storm. He hadn't realized his sexuality had been that obvious.

Two more guys and one of their wives joined the party in the front entry.

"What's going on?"

"Derek's gay," Chelsea answered flatly.

"No ... not gay." Derek pulled Liam closer to him. "I have a boyfriend. That's it."

"Sounds pretty gay." A guy he rarely spoke one-on-one with. Paul. Then Paul lifted his beer can into the air. "You want a beer, Derek?" He pointed at Liam. "And you too?"

"Would love one," Liam replied. "I'll give you a hand." He released Derek's fingers, stroked his arm, and followed Paul into the kitchen.

"We are not sticking around for this," Jackson said and grabbed Chelsea by the wrist. He tugged on her. "Come on ... we're leaving."

Chelsea broke free from his grasp. "Like hell I am." She wandered over to Tiffany. "I need to interrogate Liam. Find out why Derek has been keeping him a secret. I want details."

"Goddammit, Chelsea. You're part of the problem."

The door slammed behind Jackson after he stormed out.

Derek left the front entry and found a spot on the sofa, and settled in. Liam handed him a beer and sat beside him. It had gone better than Derek expected. The women were all fine. Even Chelsea. And three out of four guys were accepting his decision to partner up with a guy. Jackson would get over it eventually. He hoped. The random animated chatter drowned out the game.

As usual.

He watched Liam laughing and joking with Paul.

His heart fluttered.

He really did.

He really did love him.

"Is anyone going to watch this damn game?" Jessie asked as he reached for a bowl of popcorn. The hum quietened down and everyone paid attention to the television. Derek was too busy glancing over at Liam to keep track of what was happening in the game.

Liam looked at him and mouthed, "I have no idea what's going on."

Derek grinned at him. "We'll practice tackling later."

He must have said it too loud because Chelsea smacked his shoulder. "I do not need that image in my head. I'm having a hard enough time accepting that you're a couple."

"Kinda moved beyond being a couple," Liam said.

Derek's body tingled all over. They had discussed this a few nights ago. Talked about how *couple* didn't encompass what they had together. They had moved so far beyond that.

"So if you're not a couple," Chelsea said. "What are you

doing?"

Liam shrugged. "We're partners."

Chelsea crossed her arms and leaned back in her chair. "You really are in love with each other, aren't you? This isn't some kind of experiment."

"Experiment?" Derek crossed his arms, mimicking Chelsea.

"You know … trying a guy on for size to see if he fits."

"Chelsea, I've always known I was bisexual. I just needed the right guy to come along."

"And Liam. Derek. Where did you meet him?"

"At the pub," Liam interjected.

Derek grinned. "Yeah, he tried to pick me up."

"Had to do the friend thing for weeks until I wore him down," Liam said.

"And you didn't find it awkward, Derek?" Chelsea asked. "Dating a man."

"Not with Liam." Derek reached for Liam's hand. "We have so much in common."

They really did. Aside from the sporting activities they shared a passion for, they had both grown up without parents. They'd both suffered traumas while they were young.

Trauma they carried with them.

They'd bonded over it.

"What are your plans over Christmas?" Chelsea asked.

"I have to work for most of it," Liam replied. "Cancer doesn't take a holiday."

"Do you work at the cancer clinic?"

"Yes, I'm a therapy technician. I administer chemo and immunotherapy."

"How long have you done that?"

"Twelve years now."

Chelsea took a sip of her beer. "So, no Christmas plans?"

Liam nodded. "I'm going for dinner at my brother's on Christmas Day."

Chelsea looked at Derek. "And you?"

"I'm flying solo," Derek answered.

"You're not going with Liam?"

They had talked this over again—and again. Each time Liam headed to his brother's place, he promised he would tell his brother that he was bisexual. That he had a man as a partner.

Yet, each time Liam went over there, he came back and reported he'd been unable to do it. That he was too scared of losing his brother.

Christmas Day without Liam was going to be brutal.

Liam shrugged. "I haven't told my brother about Derek yet."

"Why? Are you embarrassed?" Chelsea asked.

Liam frowned. "No—not at all. I love everything about Derek." He leaned forward in his seat. "I just reconnected with my brother a couple of years ago. I'm concerned about how he'll react."

"Have you brought up LGBT stuff? Tested the water with him?"

"No ... I don't want to tip him off. He's very rigid in his thinking. I wouldn't be surprised if he leaned in the conservative direction."

Derek sighed. He got it—he did. After a lifetime apart, Liam didn't want to risk losing his brother. But how were they supposed to live a life together with him being kept hidden in the shadows? How long could that go on? Having his existence denied like that.

Chelsea shook her head. "I don't understand that. Derek is a lovely man. If he was mine, and I was in love with him, I wouldn't leave him home alone on Christmas Day."

It was just like Chelsea to be direct.

Liam rose to his feet. "I need another beer."

When he was gone, Chelsea grabbed Derek's arm. "Don't let him do that to you. Don't you dare let him pretend you don't exist. That is unacceptable."

Derek knew she was right. He knew it, but he had no recourse. Liam hadn't pressured him to come out to his friends. He was going to extend that same courtesy to Liam.

He loved him too much to push any harder than he had been already.

It was a gorgeous winter day up on the slopes of Mt. Washington. They had both managed to book New Year's Eve off work. No small feat for either one of them. They had decided to spend it snowboarding. It was their fourth trip of the season. Not as many times as they'd liked to head up to Liam's condo, but they were enjoying every minute they had up there.

Christmas Day had been odd. He and Liam had spent Christmas Eve together. Exchanged gifts, and cooked turkey dinner with all the fixings. Then they'd made love on and off for the rest of the evening. They'd curled up and fallen asleep—entwined.

Derek would've preferred it if they had lounged in bed the next morning, but Liam had to get up early to be there for his nephew opening his presents. He was out the door by 6 am.

A couple of days before Christmas, Derek had received an invite from Chelsea for Christmas Dinner on Christmas Day and he had gone. Jackson had been a bit strange, but he'd been civil.

It was a step forward.

But it had been a day of loneliness regardless. A day of sadness.

A day of feeling rejected.

Liam had decided it wouldn't be appropriate for him to tell his brother about Derek over the holidays. When Derek returned home after dinner that day, he had broken down and cried.

Desperation, frustration—and anger.

After that acknowledgment of anger, he booked in to work every evening for the next week, not wanting to leave any room to see Liam. He'd had wounds to lick, and he needed some time.

Now, things were back to normal.

He'd only been away from Liam for a week, but it had been too long.

Derek turned Liam's face toward his and kissed him. It made the chair lift sway; the shift in position. They were headed up the *Whiskey Jack* chairlift. They were sticking to blue runs today. Yesterday had included some black diamonds. They were still sore. They were going to take a run down the *Coaster*. If they felt recovered enough later, they'd agreed to check out the *Terrain Park*.

The snow was perfect. It had snowed overnight, blanketing the mountain in optimum snowboarding conditions. By the time the sun dipped, they were exhausted.

And starving.

They skidded into the Alpine Village and deposited their snowboards outside. The restaurant was filling up fast. People often stayed for dinner before driving down the mountain into town. The city of Courtenay was near the base of the mountain. If you weren't staying on the mountain, there were plenty of hotels and motels to choose from.

Tonight, though. Tonight was New Year's Eve. The mountain would be crowded for the festivities. Derek was glad they were stumbling distance from Liam's condo.

He was in the mood to celebrate.

It was their first New Year's Eve together and exactly five months since they started seeing each other. They grabbed dinner, then took turns going back to the condo to get changed.

Usually, the basic, well-used restaurant would move people on during the dinner hour, but tonight there was no risk of that. They had bought tickets for the New Year's party.

Derek slid back into the booth. They had a couple of friends with them. A straight couple they met on the slopes. They'd been standing in line with them and got to chatting. Both of them were RNs. They had a lot in common with Liam. As well as that, Chad had been a bartender while going to university. Sharon, a server. That's how the two had met. They had stories to share.

They had just finished regaling them with stories of Americans coming into the restaurant and asking if the menus and checks were in American dollars.

Derek could relate.

"So, how did you two meet," Sharon asked.

"Same as you," Derek replied. "At a pub."

Liam relayed their story. His trying to pick Derek up. Derek taking weeks to come around. How they'd kissed on their first date and how it had knocked both their socks off.

"Lust at first sight ... or love," Sharon said, smiled, and leaned on the table.

Derek snorted out a laugh. "Definitely lust."

"Us too," Chad said. "Then I got to know her. She was new to the restaurant. Working with her for months changed how I felt about her. By the time we started dating, we were already deep in each other's pockets. It was a quick step to love."

"We were pretty fast too," Liam said. "Everything about us just clicked." He pressed his shoulder to Derek's. "I love this man to pieces."

"It shows," Sharon said.

"Another round," Chad said and threw back the remainder of his beer.

Derek waved the server down.

And that's how the evening unfolded. At 9 pm, they spilled out of the pub to watch the fireworks. Then back in to do some dancing.

Derek had never been much of a dancer. He usually hung around on the outskirts of any nightclubs he had been in. He enjoyed watching *other* people move to the music.

Liam had hauled him out on the dance floor. He found himself sucking and biting his lower lip as he stared at Liam move his body to the music; his lust for the man building. He nearly groaned every time Liam hung off him or turned to press his back to Derek's chest.

That's where they were right now. Swaying on the dancefloor, Liam had the back of his head resting on Derek's shoulder. Derek's arms were around Liam's waist ... and his cock was throbbing.

He wasn't sure how much longer he could last.

When midnight hit, the kiss he gave Liam sent a clear message.

He wanted to get the hell out of there and back to the condo.

The bright winter sun streamed through the blinds of the condo. Derek rolled over and put the pillow over his head to block out the light.

"I feel sick," Liam mumbled.

"You and me both." Derek's voice was muffled by the pillow. He threw it off and onto the floor. "I need water."

"I'll come with you."

Both men struggled out of bed and headed for the kitchen. They were nude but the condo was warm. They'd accidentally left the gas fireplace on.

Liam rubbed his ass cheek as they stood in the kitchen drinking water.

"My poor ass. I can still feel you."

"Sorry about that ... I was a bit worked up." Derek grinned. "Damn, you can dance."

Liam turned on the water and filled his glass again. "Oh, hey ... forgot to tell you. I need to jam out on snowboarding next weekend. I have to go to my nephew's birthday party."

"A kid's birthday party? Why?"

Liam set the glass on the counter. "The whole family will

be there."

Derek wasn't sure if it was anger, jealousy, or anguish that fell over him. Maybe it was all three. Liam was his family. His whole damned family. They should be going to events like this together. He hated being Liam's dirty little secret.

"Not the whole family, though, is it?"

Liam crossed his arms. "Derek, we've talked about this. I'm not ready to tell my brother."

"Why? Why not? Am I not important enough to you?"

"Of course, you are."

"You're not acting like it."

"How I feel about you has nothing to do with my brother. Besides, it's none of his business."

"It should be his business. You're his little brother. You're keeping a huge part of your life from him." He couldn't stop himself from blurting it out. "And I'm losing patience with you."

If his hangover hadn't been raging, he probably would have kept it to himself. But he was suffering and resentful. He had lost the last of his restraint. And it needed to be said.

He was close to his limit.

Liam stepped toward Derek and gripped his hands. "All right. I'll tell him. After the birthday party … I'll tell him. I promise."

Derek cupped Liam's face. "Thank you." Then he kissed him.

Derek sat at home flicking through the channels on the television. Liam hadn't texted or called him. And Liam wasn't answering his attempts to contact him.

The birthday party had ended hours ago.

Maybe Liam and his brother were having a long conversation after Liam revealed he was bisexual and had a male partner. That's what they had discussed. That's what Liam was going to tell his brother and then accept whatever consequences came from that.

Liam had promised him.

His phone rang.

Liam.

"Where are you?" Derek asked. "You said you were going to come here after."

"Tired. Decided to go home."

"I was worried about you."

"Sorry."

Derek waited. Waited for Liam to say something about his discussion with his brother. Nothing. A knot formed in his gut.

"How did it go?" Derek asked.

"The party was noisy."

"Not the party. The other thing. Did you talk to your brother?"

Liam sighed. "Here's the thing, Derek. Lucas' wife Rebecca … her brother is getting married in a couple of months. It kinda dominated things."

"And, of course, you've been invited."

"Yes."

"And … you didn't tell Lucas about us."

"I couldn't. Everyone was busy talking about the wedding. It didn't seem like the right time."

"Liam, you promised me."

"I'm sorry. I'll make it up to you, I promise. I'll book

another weekend off. We can spend it together up at the mountain."

Derek felt himself retracting. "I promised to work every weekend for the next month to make up for taking New Year's Eve off.

A complete lie.

But he didn't feel like spending an entire weekend with Liam.

"What about during the week?" Liam asked.

Dammit.

"To be honest, Liam, I'm kinda off snowboarding."

"We could do something else. Just hang out in town."

Derek closed his eyes. Liam wasn't going to let up. He'd need to see him. Maybe if he did, the feelings of desperation would dissipate. Maybe their combined love would heal him.

"Tomorrow night," Derek said.

"Your place? 8?"

"Sure, yeah. I'll see you then." He had no desire to stay on the phone. "Love you."

"Love you too."

When Liam showed up at his door the next night, Liam was in tears.

He was messy sobbing.

"I'm so sorry," Liam said. "I promised you and I bailed."

"Get in here." Derek pulled Liam into the apartment and his arms. He kissed Liam's head and held him through his waves of emotion. "You're all right. I'm here. I'm not going anywhere."

"I screwed up so bad." Liam moved away. He strode

across the room. "I promised you and I totally went back on that." He looked at Derek, his gaze imploring. "I'll never do that again."

"You'll tell him before the wedding."

Derek was holding out hope that Liam would acknowledge his existence and invite him along to the wedding as his plus one. That they could attend a family event together—as partners.

"After," Liam said. "I'll tell him after."

Derek's heart sank. That was the same promise Liam had made him before going to that birthday party. Right after a significant event. Liam would tell Lucas—right after.

He had no other choice but to believe him.

"I have a special dinner planned," Derek said. "I'm making those lettuce wraps you like so much. Maybe you can help me in the kitchen."

Liam sniffed and wiped the last of his tears off his face. "I'd love that."

Making dinner together was fun. The tension between them was still there but it had eased off. After they finished eating, they found their way to each other.

The kissing turned to frantic hands. The frantic hands turned to falling into bed. The falling into bed turned to lovemaking. Afterward, they held one another.

"I'm terrified," Liam said. "What if my brother disowns me?"

"I can't tell you what you should do. All I know is from my perspective, I don't feel like we can move forward as a couple if you're hiding me from your family."

Liam kissed Derek's shoulder. "I want to choose you … I really do."

"I hate that it has to be a choice."

"That's where the world is at. Straight people have no idea what we go through."

"That's why I never wanted to date a guy," Derek said.

"The stigma?"

"Yeah. I didn't want that instability in my life. The feeling of not being safe."

"We're *not* safe."

Derek hugged Liam closer. It was true. Their love wasn't safe. Every time they went out together and even looked remotely like a couple, they ran the risk of getting beat up.

"I have no qualms about putting my life on the line for you," Derek said.

"And here I am afraid to do something simple like tell my brother about you."

Derek heaved out a sigh. "After the wedding."

"The day after … I promise."

Derek hadn't meant to but he'd tracked down Liam's brother on social media. Photos from the wedding soon started popping up on Lucas' feed and in his story. Liam looked like he was having a good time. He was incredibly handsome in his suit. Downright edible.

He looked closer at the pictures. In each, Liam was standing next to a gorgeous blonde woman. Group photos. Photo booth pictures. On the dance floor.

He leaned back and flicked back through every picture again. In every single damned picture, that woman was at Liam's side. He stopped on one picture of them on the dance floor.

They looked fucking cozy.

He was tempted to text Liam. Ask him who the hell that woman was, but he didn't want to be *that* guy. Jump to conclusions. Maybe she was one of Rebecca's many sisters.

Except she looked familiar.

Derek had expected a phone call from Liam on the night of the wedding after the festivities wrapped up. A call to calm Liam's nerves. For what lay ahead the next day. The day he would finally tell his brother about the man he was in love with.

No call.

He had a restless sleep. He wondered if Liam had slept well. Or if he'd been up most of the night. Surely, Liam would have called him if he was laying awake.

All day, Derek waited for the call from Liam. The call that would confirm Liam had kept his promise this time. That he'd chosen their love.

It was late in the evening by the time Liam called.

"How was the wedding."

"Fun."

"Your hotel?"

"Yeah, it was fine. It was nice of Rebecca's brother to cover the expense."

"Did you talk to your brother?"

Silence.

"We had early brunch with the happy couple this morning. Lunch with Rebecca's mother. My brother left after that."

"So … that's a no."

"I'm having dinner at his place next weekend. It'll be the perfect time to tell him."

Excuse after excuse. Derek felt the flush rise in his face.

He was starting to feel like Liam was never going to fully commit to him. That Liam expected him to live his life as a secret.

And who the hell was that woman?

"Who was the woman you were with?"

"What woman?"

"The one you were with in every damned picture."

"Where did you see pictures?"

"Lucas' social media."

"You were spying?"

"I was hoping to see pictures of you having fun. And you certainly were."

"You shouldn't have done that."

"Well, I did … who's the woman?"

"Her name is Pamela."

A rush of memory nearly knocked Derek off his seat. The restaurant. His date with Laura. The woman Liam had been sitting with. Liam's date for the night.

"The woman—friend you slept with?"

"Yeah … we stayed friends."

Derek's ears burned hot.

"And why did you feel the need to bring her?"

"Lucas insisted I bring a date."

"And you knew this when?"

Silence.

"Weeks ago," Liam answered.

"Why the hell didn't you tell me you were bringing her?"

"I thought it would make you mad."

Derek scoffed. "Well, you have that right." He clenched his phone. "Where did she stay?"

"Derek … look … nothing happened."

What the fuck!

Derek couldn't stop the tears. "She stayed with you … in your room?"

"Lucas expected that we were together. He booked us one room."

Derek swiped the heel of his hand across his face to clear the tears. It was pointless. They weren't going to stop anytime soon.

"You told your brother she was your girlfriend?"

Silence.

"I didn't know what else to do."

"Maybe the truth might have been an idea." Derek rolled through a sob. "I can't believe you did this to me. You're supposed to love me."

"I do … I do love you."

"Not enough."

"What the hell does that mean?"

The ache in his chest nearly doubled him over. "We're done, Liam. I'm done."

"Derek, no … please no," Liam cried. "I'll tell him … I will."

"You're too late. I can't do this anymore." Derek disconnected the call and ignored the constant stream of calls and texts from Liam. His heart broke every time the phone dinged.

He set it to mute.

Chapter Ten | Liam

Liam was frantic. Derek wasn't answering him. He had stayed up all night calling and texting. Hoping he'd wear Derek down. Let him explain. Remind Derek how much he loved him.

He had never imagined it would come to this. That Derek would break up with him. That had always been Liam's thing. Run when the relationship became serious.

Their relationship had gone way past serious and he had stayed. Stayed because he loved the man so much. He'd abandoned his old ways. He had seen a future with Derek.

Now, he'd destroyed that.

He picked up his phone.

Liam: "Derek, please. I love you."

Nothing.

Liam: "I love you more than my life. I'll do anything."

Liam: "I'll tell him. Tomorrow. I'll go to his office."

Liam: "Don't throw us away. Please."

Liam: "I'm choosing you. Please. I'm choosing you."

He wiped the tears from his eyes. He could barely see the screen.

Liam: "I would die for you, babe. I'm going to tell him."

Derek: "It has gone so far past that. You lied to me."

Oh, thank God.

Liam: "I know. I am so sorry. I didn't want to hurt you."

Derek: "You failed at that. You've crushed me."

Liam: "We didn't share the bed. Nothing happened. You have to believe me."

Derek: "At this point, I don't care if you did have sex with her."

Liam: "But I didn't. I would never do that to you."

Derek: "But you would lie about her. Tell your brother she's your girlfriend when you have a partner at home you supposedly love."

Liam: "I do. I do love you."

Derek: "Not good enough, Liam. You knew suggesting a beard would devastate me."

Liam: "It was never supposed to happen that way."

Derek: "And yet it did."

Liam: "I want to fix this."

Derek: "I don't. I'm switching my phone off."

Liam: "Please no. Derek."

Liam: "I love you. Please."

Liam: "Derek."

Nothing.

Derek had made good. He'd switched off his phone.

Liam collapsed on his bed and threw his phone at the wall. It made a cracking sound and a few bits of plastic flew off. He didn't care. Derek wasn't going to answer him anyway.

And no one else mattered.

He grabbed a pillow and sobbed into it; his tears dampening the cotton fabric of the pillowcase. He curled up his knees. His entire body was in pain.

Derek had become his entire world.

Then why hadn't he told his brother about him?

Liam rolled onto his back. Was he afraid of losing his

brother? Or was it something else? Was he afraid of the commitment? Afraid to risk everything for the man that filled his dreams?

He stared up at the ceiling. None of it mattered now. Derek had abandoned him. Like everyone else in his life. And as usual, it was his fault.

The alarm went off on his phone. He hadn't busted it completely. He needed to be at work in thirty minutes. Liam climbed off his bed. He wasn't sure how he was going to hold it together. His shift ran from 7 am until 3 pm. It would be eight long agonizing hours.

He fumbled through work in a daze, but his patients weren't compromised. He was diligent when he was with them. It was the between times. The times when he usually talked and joked around with the other technicians. He had no interest in being around people. He avoided them; his head in a book he wasn't actually reading while on his breaks.

A few people commented about his mood. Good friends. He hadn't been able to tell them about his breakup with Derek. It would make it too real. He didn't want it to be real.

He closed his eyes while sitting in his car after his shift. It was too late but he was going to do it ... he was compelled to follow through with his promise.

Liam started his car and drove to his brother's office.

Of course, his brother was busy and he had to wait in the waiting room. It was agony sitting there. He almost left on three different occasions.

"Sorry, Liam." Lucas reached for Liam's hand and shook it. "Crazy day." Liam followed Lucas down a series of corridors. "Wasn't expecting to see you again so soon."

Lucas stepped back so Liam could enter his office, then pressed the door closed behind him. "So … what brings you around?"

"I have something I want to tell you."

Lucas sat in the chair behind his desk and peaked his fingers.

"That sounds serious."

"It kinda is." Liam took a seat on the sofa situated down the window side of a very opulent office. It was a bit overwhelming. Again—he almost offered his apologies and left.

"Then, I'm listening."

Liam exhaled a deep breath. "Pamela isn't my girlfriend. She's a girl I dated a few times. It never went anywhere but we stayed friends."

"That hardly seems serious."

"There's more." Liam cleared his throat. "I date men too."

Lucas' eyebrows went up. "Men?"

"Yeah, the whole virile package."

That statement made Lucas squirm in his seat. "Why?"

"Because I'm attracted to them."

"Sexually?"

"Every way. Sexually. Personally. Everything about them."

"But you still like women?"

"I do … but I prefer men."

"You're gay."

"No. Bisexual."

"So … you're not sure."

"No, I'm sure. I'm sure I like women. But I like men

better."

"So … you'll date and sleep with both of them."

"That's the general idea of the bisexual identity." Liam looked down at his hands. "There's more. I was seeing someone for a while." He looked up at his brother. "Fell in love with him."

"In love with a man."

"Yes. His name is Derek … and he was the love of my entire existence."

"Was?"

"When he found out I took Pamela to the wedding it was the last straw for him."

"What were the other straws?"

Liam looked back at his hands. "Me not telling you about him."

"You lost him because of me?" Lucas rose from his chair and came to sit on the arm of the sofa. He put his hand on Liam's back. "You could have told me."

Liam looked up at Lucas, tears in his eyes. "I was afraid of losing you."

"Jezzus, Liam. You're an idiot if you thought that would chase me off. After I spent so much time trying to find you. You're my little brother. I'm not going to abandon you."

Lucas wrapped his arm around Liam's shoulder and hugged him.

"Dumbass," Lucas whispered.

It made Liam smirk and lean heavily into Lucas' embrace. His big brother was accepting him. Every damned bit of him. His smirk slipped from his face. Losing Derek could have been avoided. He should have taken that risk. His love for Derek had been worth taking that risk.

A lifetime with Derek was worth any risk.

He'd really fucked things up.

"What am I going to do?" Liam asked.

"About Derek?"

"How do I get him back?"

"Lies are pretty hard to come back from. Especially big ones." Lucas leaned away and looked at Liam. "Jeezus, I put the two of you in the same hotel room."

"We worked it out. I slept on the floor."

"Does Derek know you shared the room?"

Liam nodded. "Yup. He figured it out."

"I don't know, Liam. I don't know how you're going to come back from this."

"I big time betrayed him, didn't I?"

"In a rather unforgivable way."

Liam leaned forward and put his head in his hands. "I'm never going to recover."

"You will. It might take a while, but you will."

Liam looked at Lucas. "I love him so much." Head back in his hands. "Like so much … thinking about living my life without him is ripping my soul out. I started having dreams about spending forever with him. Growing old together. All of it."

"You were in deep."

"So deep." Liam leaned against the back of the sofa and stared at the wall. "I'll never find anyone like him ever again." He threw his hands up. "That's it. I'm done. I'm going to spend the rest of my life having meaningless sex. I'm done with relationships."

"That's a bit severe."

Liam stared at Lucas. "You don't understand. He's *it* for

me. The only one I want."

"So … what are you going to do about it?"

Liam pinched his eyebrows. "What do you mean?"

"How are you going to get him back?"

"If that's even possible, I wouldn't know where to start."

"Think about it. I'm sure you'll figure something out."

Liam rose and reached for Lucas' hand to shake it. Lucas nudged his hand away and brought Liam in for a hug. "I know you can do this. I can't wait to meet him "

Liam wandered out of Lucas' office and looked up the street. He was only six blocks away from the pub Derek worked in. As if compelled, he started for it. Just to catch a glimpse of him. Even if it was only for a moment. He needed to see him.

He walked through the doors. The hostess greeted him and brought him to a stool at the bar. Derek was nowhere to be seen. The bartender was a woman he'd seen before.

"What I get you, hun," she asked.

"Gin and tonic. And hey, is Derek working today?"

"Lost track of your boyfriend's schedule?"

Liam swallowed hard. "We're not together anymore."

The woman frowned. "Oh, I'm so sorry to hear that. You were making Derek crazy happy. Never seen that guy smile so much." She looked at her phone. "He'll be here any minute."

When the drink was set in front of Liam, he slammed it back and ordered another. His nerves were sending off absolute panic sparks in all directions.

Then he saw him. The man he wanted to spend eternity with.

Derek's brow furrowed hard when he was Liam. He

headed straight for him.

"What the hell are you doing here? This is my place of work."

"You wouldn't answer your phone." Liam reached across the bar. "And I need to talk to you. I've been going out of my mind. I've never regretted anything so much in my life."

"You lied to me. You kept it from me … that you were bringing that woman with you."

"I didn't want to upset you."

"You had no right to decide that for me. You should have told me what you were planning and we could have discussed it together … because that's what partners do." Derek exhaled hard. "You thought I'd never see those pictures. Would you have told me if I hadn't seen them?"

Liam stared at his drink. He would have kept the whole business a secret. He would've hung on to the guilt of what he'd done. It probably would have undone them eventually.

He shook his head, no.

"Well, there you have it. You were prepared to keep it from me for the rest of our lives. Is that what you're telling me?"

The other bartender, the woman, touched Derek's shoulders. "I'll cover you until you're done here if you like."

"No need." Derek threw his bar towel over his shoulder. "I'm done."

Liam slipped off the barstool. It was pointless. He'd fucked up so badly there was no going back. One simple, stupid decision and he'd brought his entire future to an end.

One last thing he needed to know.

"Do you still love me?" Liam wasn't sure why he needed to know that. Maybe to hang on to a bit of hope—that there was a possibility of reconciliation.

Derek gripped the bartop; his eyes brimming with tears.

"I'm honestly walking a thin line between love and hate," he replied.

Liam couldn't stop himself. He crumpled to his knees on the floor. It felt like someone had stabbed him in the heart. Derek didn't move—just stared at him; tears running down his cheeks.

Liam stumbled to his feet. He needed to get out of there. *Hate.*

He didn't know if he could continue to live if Derek hated him.

He careened down the street toward his apartment. His feet had never felt so heavy. Each breath was unwelcome.

He wanted to curl up somewhere and die.

Chapter Eleven | Derek

Derek crouched down behind the bar to catch his breath and wipe away the tears coating his cheeks. He had an eight-hour shift in front of him. He couldn't afford to fall apart.

Susie touched his shoulder. "Do you need a minute? I can cover you."

Even though their dating life had come to a fiery end, Susie and he had remained friends. He appreciated the offer. He nodded, rose to his feet, and headed for the staff room.

There, he found Richard getting ready for his shift.

"Woah." Richard put his hand on Derek's shoulder. "What the hell happened to you?"

"Liam." It was all the words he could get out.

"He broke up with you."

Derek shook his head. "No. I did."

Richard's eyebrows rose. "That's a new twist." He sat on an old, worn chair. "He wouldn't have cheated on you if that's what you suspect. That's just not something he would do."

"No, I know that."

Richard waggled his finger in the air. "His long lost brother. He still wouldn't tell him, right? We had that problem. Drove me crazy."

"That's part of it."

"What's the rest?"

Derek crossed his arms. "He took a woman to a family

wedding without telling me."

Richard frowned. "Jeezus, what the hell was he thinking?"

"Right?"

"I'm sure he didn't do it maliciously. Probably trying to protect you by not telling you."

"Don't make excuses for him. We should have discussed it before he went off and did it."

Richard sighed. "Where were you in your relationship?"

"We were in love. We were headed toward a future together."

Richard squirmed in his seat. "Liam actually told you he loved you?"

"All the time."

"Wow … okay. And you threw that away for one stupid mistake?"

"It was a big fucking mistake."

"Still." Richard pursed his lips. "So … you're sure you'll find love like that again."

Derek pinched up his face. "What? Of course not."

"Then I don't get it."

"He lied to me."

"And is that a habit of his?"

"I have no idea. He never kept his promises about telling his brother?"

"That's not the same as lying." Richard rose. "I can tell you from experience, lying is not something Liam does. He's honest to a fault. He was off the rails when he lied to you. It must be eating him up inside. I can almost guarantee you, he'll never do it again."

Derek huffed out a breath. He knew what Richard was

saying was true. Liam wasn't a liar. That's why it had caught him so off guard. And he thought they were so much further in their relationship than that. That Liam could come to him with anything.

Derek waved to Richard as Richard left the room.

That's what was throwing him. That Liam hadn't trusted him enough to come to him with his dilemma. That Liam hadn't trusted him enough to believe they could work it out together.

He sat in the chair Richard had vacated and put his head in his hands.

It was no wonder Liam had trouble trusting people. Look at his childhood. Being bounced from house to house. Each new house promised to take care of him, then shipped him off when he was just being himself. Just being a kid. His upbringing had been devoid of trust—and love.

Trust would still take some time.

But Liam's love for him was abundant and pure.

"Dammit," Derek whispered.

He needed to finish his shift, then he needed to find Liam.

Derek kept pressing the button, but Liam didn't answer the buzzer at his apartment building. And he wasn't responding to any text messages or calls. He could be sleeping but Derek had stayed overnight many times at Liam's place. That buzzer was bloody loud. There was no way anyone could sleep through it. It was 2 in the morning and Liam should have been home by now.

He ran a hand through his hair and paced up and down the sidewalk outside the building. He had no idea where

Liam could be. It wouldn't be like him to find a bar to crawl into until the early morning hours. Liam wasn't much of a drinker. But maybe if he was upset.

Derek stopped his pacing.

Fuck, I hope not.

He raced around to the back of the building where the shed was located. He lifted the rock the key was kept under and opened the shed door. He nearly fell to his knees.

Liam's kayak was gone.

It was the middle of February. In the middle of the night.

Where the hell did you go?

There was only one place Derek could think of. The place where they had first whispered words of love to each other. Out in the middle of the ocean. The island.

He needed to get home. Get his kayak, go after him, and bring him home where it was warm. Liam would freeze to death out in the elements.

Maybe that's what he wants.

And whose fault is that?

Derek rushed back to his car and took off. Forty minutes later, he was looking out at the dark water. He peered back over his shoulder. Liam's car was sitting in the parking lot.

He pushed his kayak into the water and braved the icy cold water seeping into his winter boots before he jumped in and pushed off. Even with his thickest parka and snowboarding pants on, he was shivering within minutes of getting out there. After a kilometer of paddling, the heat from his body smoothed things out. He stopped shaking. He dug hard to get across the water. As expected, Liam's kayak was pulled up on the sandy beach of the island.

He scrambled up the hill and ducked through the trees,

headed straight for where they had camped together. As Derek got closer, he could see the orange glow of a fire.

Derek stepped into the small clearing. Liam was lying in a sleeping bag facing the fire. His eyes were closed. They popped open when Derek scuffed up to where he was lying.

"What the fuck?" Liam struggled inside his sleeping bag, then freed himself and sat up. "How the hell did you get here? It's the middle of the night."

"I rowed … same as you … in the dark."

"Why? You're done with me, remember."

"Because I realized something." Derek sat on the ground with his back to the fire. There was only one thing on his mind for the entire rowing experience over there. One thing he needed to say. "You, Liam Hedley, are the man I want to spend the rest of my life with."

Liam's brow dipped. "But what I did. You'd have to forgive what I did."

Derek sighed. "Already done. Thought about it my whole shift. You had your reasons for doing what you did. I don't agree with them, and I wish you had come to me before you did it, but I know you didn't do it to hurt me. But you have to realize something … you can trust me. I walked away but I came back. I'll always come back. I'll never abandon you—never."

"That's a hard thing for me to believe."

Derek reached for and took Liam's hand. "I know. And we'll work on that … together."

"I'll never do anything like that again."

"I know."

"So, that's it?" Liam jerked, then started crying. He covered his eyes with one hand as his body shook. "You've come back ... you've come back to me?"

"I never left. Not really. I was always going to find my way back to you." Derek sat beside Liam. He wrapped his arm around Liam's shoulder and tugged him in close. "Always."

Liam leaned into Derek's embrace. "I thought you were gone forever."

"I love you too much to walk away from you."

"I am so sorry for everything. Not telling my brother. Pamela. All of it."

"I know."

Liam sniffed. "I told my brother."

Derek shifted and looked over at Liam. "You did? When?"

"After my shift yesterday."

"But we'd broken up."

"Felt like I should keep my promise to you."

"And what did he say?" Derek wasn't sure he wanted to know. He did know that if it was bad news, they would deal with it together.

"He said I could have told him sooner. That's he's fine with it." Liam nuzzled his cheek against Derek's shoulder. "He wants to meet you."

"Why would he assume he'd get to meet me?"

"He was pretty confident we'd work it out." Liam gripped Derek's arm. "I told him how much I loved you ... that you loved me too. I told him you were the love of my entire existence."

"What does that mean ... entire existence?"

"It means, I don't want anyone else ... ever. You're *it* for me. You're my forever love."

"Dammit, Liam." Derek turned and cradled Liam's face and brought their lips together. He felt like he would melt and become one with the man he loved. That's what he wanted. To never be separated from him again. To be part of him. Their lips parted. "Honestly, what does that mean? I need to know what you're thinking."

"It means I want to commit to you," Liam replied. His breath helped to warm the small space between them. He clung to Derek's hands.

"Like marriage?"

Liam shook his head. "Yes, but no. We don't need that." He looked at the fire. "Let's do it right here in front of this fire. Make a commitment to each other. A forever bond."

Forever.

Derek stared at the fire. It's what he wanted. More than anything, it was what he wanted. A lifetime with Liam. A forever. But pledging his commitment right now? Out in the wilderness? Alone. Just the two of them. Without a moment to even think about it?

He made his decision.

He loved this man more than he'd felt his heart was capable of.

"We told each other we loved one another on this island," he said. "Seems like the right place to take this next step. Let's do it. Affirm our commitment. I want this for us."

Liam shuffled up onto his knees and faced Derek. "Get up on your knees."

Derek did as instructed. Rose onto his knees and faced Liam. They grabbed each other's gloved hands. "Wait." Derek stripped his gloves off. "Take your gloves off."

Liam removed his gloves and set them on the ground

beside him, then took Derek's hands. The skin-on-skin contact was important to Derek. There could be no barrier between them.

"What do we say?" Derek asked.

"Um … maybe start at the beginning." Liam cleared his throat. "Derek Laney. From the first day we spoke, I knew there was something special about you. That you would bring out something in me I never knew existed. An ability to love another human being fully and completely.

"I never imagined you'd build a bridge for me to walk across—to trust. But you did. I'm still walking that bridge but I know you are walking right alongside me. And you've nurtured a belief that any words you spoke to me are true. When you told me you loved me, I knew in my soul that those words weren't lies. Every single day with you has been a joy as you proved it.

"I see my entire future with you. We are going to be there to support and love each other through every stage of our lives. I can feel it in my heart. I love you, Derek, and I want to spend the rest of my life with you by my side."

Derek released Liam's hand and tried, unsuccessfully, to clear the tears from his cheeks. "Wow … okay. How to follow that." He took a deep breath, released it, and gazed into Liam's eyes.

"Liam Hedley. When I first met you, I was annoyed." He smiled. "But just for a moment. I wasn't sure why you were talking to me but you intrigued me. Your eyes … sucked me right in. And your smile … like electricity on my skin. When you touched me, then moved away, it felt like my world sunk into darkness. I didn't know it then, but I was in deep already.

"Every day after that I spent in your company, my affection for you grew. When you implied a date, I was so ready, but the kiss threw me off. It scared me how much you had come to mean to me. How much that kiss felt so right. How I so badly wanted to do it again—and never stop."

Derek licked his lips. "Our first time together in bed … I knew. I knew I wasn't getting out of there unscathed. That our relationship was going places." He closed his eyes. "Then I fell in love with you." He opened them again and drank in the look of love on Liam's face.

"When that happened, my entire world clicked into place. I knew I never wanted to be without you. When you told me you loved me … oh, my god. My heart swelled with love, joy—relief. I knew we were in this together. That together we'd figure everything out.

"Our emotions. Our path. Our future together. I knew I'd never be alone again. I love you, Liam, and I want to spend the rest of my life with you by my side."

Liam lifted their clasped hands and wiped a streak of tears from his cheek. He laughed nervously and smiled. "What do we do now?"

"I think we should seal it with a kiss."

Liam leaned in and Derek met him. Their lips greeted each other with more than love. More than desire. A promise. The kiss was a promise to each other. That they'd never part.

When they separated, their eyes were glassy—cheeks damp.

Derek shivered. It was damn cold out. Even in front of the fire.

"I need to get these wet boots off," he said.

"God, yeah." Liam scooted back to give Derek room. "I don't want to lose you so soon after we've taken commitment vows. I'd rather we had a long life together."

"Help me with these." Derek sat back and Liam yanked the boots off his feet. Then his socks. Liam put the socks on a couple of rocks surrounding the fire to dry and the opening of the boots tipped toward the heat. Then, he fully unzipped his sleeping bag.

"Come under here." Liam arranged the sleeping bag on the ground and held the loose end up for Derek to fit in beside him. "We'll have to wait until sunrise to paddle back."

"I hope you have more wood."

Liam pointed at a pile of firewood on the far side of the fire. "Plenty."

Even with the fire, the night was cold. They managed to nod off a few times, but sitting up—sleep didn't come to them. They didn't dare lie down. The ground was too cold.

The paddle back across to Oak Bay took longer than usual because they were exhausted and cold. Their kayaks loaded onto their cars, then stood across from each other.

"I need sleep. Gonna head to my place," Liam said.

"Yeah, me too. We can meet up later."

Derek stepped forward and wrapped Liam up in his arms. There was something he wanted. Now that they'd taken vows, there was something that didn't make sense.

"I want you to move in with me," he said.

Liam's eyebrows rose. "Are you sure?"

Derek laughed. "Of course, I'm sure. We've just taken vows. It doesn't make sense for us to live in two different places."

"Okay, but I'd like to keep my apartment."

Why?

"In case it doesn't work out?" Derek furrowed his brow.

"No. The rent there is awesome and we might decide we want to live in Chinatown someday. And I don't want to get rid of my furniture. I really like it. Took me years to collect what I have. Plus … maybe we'll move into a house someday and need it."

"Okay. You could sublet your apartment."

"Exactly. Then we won't be spending any extra money."

We.

The sound of that word rolling off Liam's tongue gave Derek shivers. They were really doing this. They had taken vows and they were moving in together.

They were starting a life together.

Derek cupped Liam's face in both hands and kissed him.

"I'm going to have trouble sleeping," he said.

"I think you'll find you're wrong about that. I'm beyond exhausted. I'm sure you are too. I need a hot shower and at least 12 hours of shut-eye."

"Can I come over tomorrow morning and help you pack?"

"Yeah." Liam smiled. "I'm not working. We can do that."

"Okay." Derek grinned. "Okay. We have a plan."

Liam smirked. "Yes, we do. I'm moving in." He kissed Derek. "See you tomorrow."

"Can't wait."

They were reluctant to part but eventually did. As Derek drove home, he couldn't stop smiling. The man he loved with his whole heart was going to be living with him—like true partners.

He looked at his left hand. He felt like the vow should be signified somehow.

When he got home, he sent Liam a text.

Derek: "Do we want rings?"

Liam: "Like wedding rings?"

Derek: "Yeah. I want everyone to know I found my forever person."

Liam: <smiley emoji> I'd love that.

Derek: "Tomorrow after we drop off your stuff at my place?"

Liam: "Perfect." <heart emoji>

Derek: "Okay. Going to say goodnight. Love you."

Liam: "Love you too. Goodnight."

Derek curled up in bed. He wished Liam was with him but in another day, he'd be waking up with Liam every day. He held that thought in his head as he fell asleep.

Chapter Twelve | Liam

Liam had trouble falling asleep, he was so excited. Tomorrow he was going to be packing up his clothes, bathroom stuff, favorite things, and a few kitchen items he couldn't live without.

And he'd be moving the whole lot over to Derek's.

He lay in bed and held his left hand up in the air so he could look at it.

Tomorrow, he'd have a ring on that finger. White gold or silver. With a tiny diamond chip. That's what he wanted. He rolled onto his side and closed his eyes. Never in his thirty-six years had he ever imagined he'd one day be looking forward to shopping for a commitment ring.

Tomorrow.

His world was going to change tomorrow.

He fell asleep around 9 in the morning and he woke around 6 pm, stumbled into the kitchen, made some mac and cheese, then parked himself in front of the television. He'd go back to bed in a couple of hours. Let his body recover from the night sitting up in the freezing cold.

It still felt like the cold was in his bones. He finished his dinner and headed for the shower. He cranked up the heat on the water and stepped in under the torrent of glorious warmth.

He stayed in there for a good twenty minutes; just standing there. He thought about Derek, the vows, the emotion on Derek's face as he'd said his vows. It had all been true. Liam could see it in his eyes. That amazing man loved him. He'd vowed to never leave his side.

A crazy, intense smile broke out across Liam's face.

He nearly swooned.

And his eyes. Derek's eyes. The joy in them had been complete. Even in the firelight, he'd seen it. It had nearly done his heart in to see Derek so happy.

Liam turned off the water and toweled off. He went straight to bed and hauled the comforter over his shoulders. He couldn't keep his eyes open to stay awake any longer.

He pictured Derek's eruption of joy as he fell asleep.

Derek was there early. They'd both slept more than 12 hours and were ready to get going. Liam had been up since 6, sorting through his clothes. He didn't have any boxes other than the plastic bins he had stored out in the shed. He'd brought them in and started filling them.

He had more clothes than Derek had been expecting.

"So glad I have a 2-bedroom apartment," Derek said. "We're going to need that second closet to house all your clothes. It can be your glorified dressing room."

Liam grinned. "Works for me." He shoved the last of his pants into a bin. They wouldn't be putting lids on the bins. They were full to overflowing. Liam headed for the living room, first stopping at the front entry to pick up the newspaper he had collected to wrap breakables in.

"What's out here?" Derek asked.

"Just a few trinkets. Little things I've picked up along the way." He lifted a red, toy fire engine. It was cast iron with plastic wheels. "This stayed with me the whole time I was growing up. It was the one thing I was able to hide away with my clothes so no one would take it."

Derek stroked Liam's arm. "You didn't have toys?"

"Not really." Liam shrugged. "Every time I was moved on, there was no room to take anything I had been given for my birthday ... Christmas, whatever. Just my clothes and a few small things." He turned the truck over in his hands. "Pretty sure my mom gave me this."

"We'll find a great spot for it. I promise. And anything else you want to bring."

There were only a handful of things. His fire truck, a ceramic horse, and a worn copy of a book he had read so many times as a child that he had it memorized. Other than that, there was only kitchen stuff. He wasn't going anywhere without his Dutch oven and favorite frying pan.

He packed everything into the top half of the last bin. He put the lid on this one to protect his treasures. Liam looked around the apartment. Everything else was part of the décor. He liked everything but had no particular attachment to it. It would be fine to sublet as is.

Luckily, Derek had borrowed a pick-up truck from a friend. They loaded everything into the back and drove the short distance to Derek's apartment; the whole ride over holding hands.

Two days ago, Liam's world had been coming to a crashing end. He had felt he couldn't go through with another day. He had headed to the island partly to feel closer to Derek. Partly to let the elements have their way with him. He hadn't wanted to die—just to suffer physically. He'd wanted a tangible manifestation of the pain he was feeling in his mind and heart.

It took them twenty minutes to load everything into Derek's apartment.

"Should we break for lunch, then look for those rings?" Derek asked as he collapsed onto the sofa. "I'm starving. I didn't eat breakfast. Wanted to get over to your place first thing."

"Sounds like a plan." Liam dropped down beside Derek. He reached for and touched Derek's thigh. "Do you know where you want to go for the rings?"

"I have a place in mind. I did some research last night."

"Downtown?"

"Yeah. You wanna grab some bao?"

"It's still early. I'm thinking waffles."

"Mm … yeah. Good thinking."

"Do you want to walk?"

Derek looked out the window. "The sun seems to be holding. We can bundle up. A walk would do us both good. I was in the bedroom for so long, it's like I was hibernating."

"Me too." Liam rose to his feet. "Let's do this."

"Are you as excited as I am?" Derek led the way into the elevator and pressed the number for the first floor. "About getting rings?"

Liam leaned against Derek and wrapped his hand around Derek's arm. He clung to him and lay his head on Derek's shoulder. "So excited."

"I wish we'd recorded ourselves saying our vows. Something to look back on."

"I'll never forget the words you spoke to me."

Derek kissed Liam's head. "Me either."

The elevator doors opened and a couple stood just outside. Derek didn't step away from Liam. In fact, he placed his hand on Liam's hand to keep it clinging to his arm.

Liam hummed with satisfaction. Things were going to be different. He could feel it. Derek was proud to be with him. Derek loved him and wanted everyone to know it.

Derek released him and slipped his hand into Liam's. They walked the whole way downtown like that; hand in hand. They received a few odd looks but nothing malicious.

They arrived at the waffle house unscathed. They must have been looking at each other with longing and love in their eyes because the server piped up with a question.

"Are you celebrating anything special today? An anniversary perhaps?"

Liam smiled at her. "We had a commitment ceremony night before last."

"Ah." She nodded and smiled. "I knew something was going on. Congratulations."

"Thank you," Derek said. "Best night of my life."

"I'll bet." Then she shifted back to business mode. "What can I get you two?"

"An order of caramelized banana waffles," Liam said.

"Me too." Derek handed the menus to the server. He turned his attention back to Liam. "I've been thinking about the rings. I want something plain. Just a silver band."

"I'm looking for something a bit more than that. I like the idea of a diamond."

"I don't need one. You're my diamond."

Liam smirked. "Aren't we mushy this morning."

Derek reached for Liam's hand and stroked the top of it with his thumb once he had it in his. "Every day. I want you to know how special you are to me."

"I feel it from you. Every action. Every word. Every moment I'm with you."

A middle-aged woman approached their table; her face screwed up tight and red.

"You're disgusting," she hissed. "The two of you … you're an abomination."

Derek squeezed Liam's hand. He could feel the tension building in Derek's body.

Don't engage.

Just don't engage.

"I'll have you know, I love this man," Derek said.

Okay. Derek was going to engage.

"I love him and I want to spend the rest of my life with him," Derek continued. "If you think that is so wrong, you need to examine yourself and your morals … very carefully."

"My morals are fine. I'm a Christian."

"Then you're reading the bible wrong," Liam chimed in. "Maybe start again."

The woman grunted, then left them alone.

Liam sighed as he looked at Derek. "You all right?"

"First time for everything. Never been verbally attacked by a homophobe before."

"Thankfully it doesn't happen often."

Derek laid his other hand on top of their clasped ones. "Now, about those rings."

Liam liked that Derek was able to shift gears so easily. The woman hadn't rattled him. He'd dealt with her and moved on. They had more important things on their minds.

Namely, their love.

"Tell me more about every moment we're together

meaning something to you," Derek said. "How can I make you feel even more special?"

"Well …." Liam smirked. He was about to engage in some dirty talk when the food arrived.

The waffles were amazing—as usual. They waddled out of there full of perfectly cooked Belgium waffles, heaps of caramelized bananas, and more whipped cream than should be legal.

The jewelry store wasn't far away. A few blocks. A little rush of apprehension rippled through Liam's body as Derek rang the buzzer to be let in.

This was a massive step. Commitment vows and rings. He had never thought this would be in his future. That he would have a partner he wanted to spend forever with.

He spotted the exact ring he was looking for. According to the jeweler it was made from sapphire tungsten and had a .06-carat diamond. Liam slipped it on. The sizing was perfect.

"What do you think, Derek?"

Derek took his hand and held it. "It looks good on you." He brushed his thumb over it. "Maybe we should have the same one." He turned to the jeweler. "Do you have another one?"

"As luck would have it, we do." The jeweler stepped through into a back room. He returned with an assortment of sizes for the same ring. Derek tried them on until he found one that fit.

A rush of butterflies fluttered in Liam's stomach as they held their hands up together—side by side. This was real. This was really happening.

Derek turned to face Liam. He glanced over at the

jeweler. "We'll take them." He brushed his fingers down Liam's cheek. "I love you." Then he kissed him.

Liam supported himself by clutching to Derek's shoulder. They were in a non-queer public space and Derek was kissing him. He realized he was nearly over the bridge when it came to trust in Derek. The man he loved was making his love known to the world. Without compromise.

"I love you too." He gripped Derek's hands. "I can't wait to show everyone." Liam stepped away and removed his wallet from his coat pocket. "We'll pay for each other's."

Derek laughed. "They're the same price."

"It's the thought."

The walk home was full of excitement. Talking, laughing, and shoving each other playfully.

Home.

He was walking home.

Home with Derek.

They spent thirty minutes tops putting all of Liam's clothes away. There was a lot of it but he'd kept it on hangers. It was easy to hang up everything.

Liam walked around the living room, looking for places to put his treasures. A bookcase provided the perfect place. Derek had told him to put his things wherever he wanted.

His eyebrows dipped. There was a picture of a young boy and an adolescent girl on one of the shelves. They were seated on a bed. The girl was wearing a pink kerchief.

He suspected the boy was Derek. Who was the girl?

"Fucking hell … this thing weighs a ton," Derek shouted from the kitchen.

Dutch oven.

"You'll thank me when I make roast beef in it."

"Yum." Derek swept up behind Liam and wrapped him up in his arms, chest to back, his chin resting on Liam's shoulder. "I love your cooking."

"I like when we cook together."

"That can be arranged on the nights we're both home."

Liam frowned. There were going to be lots of nights when he'd be alone. Derek often worked nights. He only ever worked days. Now that he wasn't dating anymore, he'd be relying on his friends for things to do. Derek hugged him closer. Liam smiled. He'd manage.

"What do you want to do now?" Liam asked. "I won't want to eat for a while. Those waffles will have me filled up until Christmas rolls around again."

"We can have a late dinner. Just a salad or something." Derek kissed the side of Liam's neck. "You know what we haven't done since taking our vows?"

Liam smirked. "Pray tell."

"We have not consummated this union of ours."

Liam's cock paid attention to those words. He'd been thinking about it on and off all day. When they'd be able to join together intimately as true life partners.

"What did you have in mind?" Liam teased.

"I was thinking of taking you to *our* bedroom and ravishing you."

Our bedroom.

"I can get behind that idea." Liam tipped his head as Derek licked and sucked his neck. He shivered as Derek's teeth scraped across his skin; each nip escalating his arousal. Derek kissed the top of his spine, then switched sides until Liam was trembling with desire.

"Enough," Liam whispered. He turned to face Derek and

engulfed Derek's mouth with his own. Wave after wave, he captured every taste—every sound. He cupped Derek's face and stayed in those undulate moments for a while. It was only days ago when he thought he'd never kiss Derek's lips again. To be able to do so now … he was going to revel in it.

Derek pulled away, took Liam's hand, and led him into *their* bedroom. Liam hadn't been in there yet. They'd put all of his clothes away in the second bedroom.

He stopped and stared.

The bed was covered in red rose petals. He nearly teared up. It was beautiful—the display. The thought behind it. The intention of what they'd be doing on it. Derek had even changed the duvet cover out for a winter white one. The contrast with the petals was stunning.

"Derek … it's incredible."

"More incredible with you on it."

Derek lifted Liam's shirt off over his head. Then eased his pants and underwear off his hips. Liam stepped out of them and his socks, mesmerized by the entire experience.

"Lie down," Derek said. "I want to see you on those petals."

A rush of crimson colored Liam's cheeks. He'd never been gazed upon in the nude before. Sure, he'd been naked in front of lots of people. This felt different. Derek wanted to admire him.

Admire—and love him unconditionally.

As Liam arranged himself, Derek removed his clothes.

His cock was hard; his hand stroked it.

Liam placed his head on the pillows and stretched his arms up above his head. He draped them atop his hair—

offering Derek full access to an area he loved. He kept his legs crossed at the ankles.

The petals felt luxurious beneath his back and his ass, and the back of his thighs. Derek watched him, his eyes nearly unblinking. His lips parted.

"God, you're gorgeous," Derek whispered, then leaned against the end of the bed and uncrossed Liam's legs. He kissed the inside of each ankle—then licked them.

Little tendrils of passion shot up Liam's legs straight to his cock.

Derek bent his ankle up and kissed the bottom of Liam's left foot. This was going to be drawn out and sexually agonizing. And Liam couldn't be more thrilled by the prospect.

They had all the time in the world together.

Chapter Thirteen | Derek

The soles of Liam's feet were salty and musky from his winter boots. Derek hummed against one, making Liam squirm. They were heavenly. His skin was smooth and tight. His toes, responsive. Liam shivered each time he took a new one into his mouth and played with it with his tongue; circling—sucking. He licked the top of Liam's foot, then kissed his shin.

He was going to work up one side of Liam and down the other. He kissed his knee, then his thigh, then his inner thigh—his cheek and stubble brushed against Liam's stiff cock. Then his hip. His waist. His chest. He circled one of Liam's nipples with his tongue, then sucked it into his mouth. Gentle—loving. He kissed his collarbone, then nuzzled his underarm and neck.

He teased Liam as he brushed his lips across Liam's—featherlight.

Derek started down the other side. Liam writhed and pressed his hands to the headboard above him as Derek tortured him. Derek smirked as he skimmed from place to place.

His objective—to drive Liam to absolute carnal distraction.

Traveling.

A final kiss on the bottom of Liam's right foot.

His journey complete, Derek surged up between Liam's

legs and took his cock into his mouth. Liam's hips rose—his ass clenched. His legs fell open. Derek stroked Liam's length with his tongue and lips. He paid attention to the tension building in Liam's body. He didn't want him to cum yet.

There—right there.

Derek released him and tucked Liam's legs back together. Derek straddled Liam's thighs and shifted until he was over Liam's hips. He placed both hands on Liam's chest.

There was a silent exchange between them.

Derek reached back and guided Liam's bare cock to his hole. It felt so different than a cock packed into a smooth, tight condom as it pierced his ring of muscle. Derek held the shaft firm as he descended on it. Liam tipped his head back and groaned as Derek came to rest on his hips.

Brushing his fingers across Liam's lips, Derek gazed down at him. He bent forward and kissed him—soft but urgent. He sat straight up and rose and fell on Liam's cock, his own hard length bobbing in the air. His powerful thighs carried him up and down. He rolled his head back as a swell of incredible pleasure flowed through him. His gut tightened. He needed to hold out.

He gazed down at Liam. He sensed the telltale signs that Liam was about to come. His eyes closed and his mouth popped open, and his breathing quickened.

Derek touched his face. "I want you to fill me."

Liam's eyes fluttered open and he grasped Derek's hips. He licked his lips and jerked upward, grunting. Derek's chest expanded as he rode through the life-changing experience. Liam filling him—claiming him as the man he was going to spend the rest of his life with.

He sat there a moment, basking in the oneness.

Derek pulled off Liam and edged in between Liam's legs. Liam adjusted his position and wrapped his legs around Derek's waist. Derek stroked his cock a few times then edged his way into Liam. The warmth, the velvety softness—it was surreal. Skin-on-skin, they became one again.

He was tender and measured; each thrust containing so much meaning. Liam sighed and gasped beneath him, his hips rocking to take Derek all the way in each time.

Liam raked his hands into Derek's hair.

"I love you," he whispered. "Make me yours—always and forever yours."

Derek increased his pace as the coil controlling his release tightened—then sprung loose. He spilled into Liam; each gentle thrust gliding through the slickness.

He collapsed atop Liam and sought out his mouth.

There was a connection there that had never been there before. It was like taking their commitment vows all over again. They'd partaken in an act of total and complete trust.

He rolled off Liam and held him.

Liam kissed his chin and spoke the words confirming it.

"I trust you completely," Liam said.

"I wasn't sure. I took a chance suggesting no condoms."

"I was ready."

Derek brushed some hair off Liam's forehead so he could see him better. "I needed to feel that—to know that feeling. To stay connected with you even after we finished."

Liam smiled. "Well, we've certainly accomplished that." He brushed his fingers up and down Derek's arm. "Never again with the condoms … promise me."

Derek shook his head. "No intention of going back."

Liam snuggled in against him. "My brother and his wife want to meet you. I texted him while you were in the washroom at the waffle house. To let him know we're back together."

Back together.

It was so much more than back together.

Derek stroked the ring on Liam's finger. "Did you tell him about the vows?"

"No, I thought I'd surprise him."

In Derek's experience, surprises like this didn't tend to go over well with families. When he had eloped with his girlfriend and come back married, her parents and siblings had thrown a fit. They had wanted to be there for the big day. He'd regretted their decision to exclude them.

This was different, though. Their ceremony had more meaning because there was no doubt in his mind they'd spend an entire life together—just them. Those vows had been private.

"When am I meeting them?" Derek asked.

"Tomorrow night … unless that doesn't work. Are you working?"

"I can have someone cover my shift."

"Perfect. Dinner and drinks after they put Cameron to bed."

Derek's brow dipped. "Forgot about your nephew."

Liam put his hand on Derek's shoulder. "You don't want kids, do you?"

That's probably something they should have discussed before committing to each other. Kids were practically a deal breaker. He'd adjust if Liam wanted them, though. But only for Liam.

But the truth was …

"No," Derek said. "I have no interest in having kids."

Liam smiled. "Oh, thank God … me either."

Derek exhaled long and slow.

Disaster averted.

"Wouldn't that be weird, though," Liam said. "If we just got each other pregnant."

Derek laughed. "*You're* weird."

"Let's go with quirky."

Quirky and gorgeous. Tender and caring. Giving, humorous, and intelligent. Liam was all of those things. He brushed his fingers along Liam's eyebrow as he gazed into Liam's eyes. He'd be waking up to those inquisitive gray-blue eyes every single day for the rest of his life.

He couldn't imagine a life better than that.

"When I first met you," Liam said. "There was no light—no joy in your eyes. Even when you smiled, there was such sadness about you."

"You asked me about that during our trip to Tofino."

"And you evaded the question."

"There was no question … just an observation. But you know why. Growing up with my grandparents wasn't easy. Plus, I lost my dog six months before that."

Liam sighed. "Then who's the girl in the picture?"

Derek frowned. It was bound to come up eventually. He hadn't hidden the picture away. He had wanted Liam to spot it. He had wanted Liam to be the one to bring up her existence.

Derek looked down between them. "Julie. My big sister."

"Cancer?"

"Leukemia."

"How old was she?"

"Twelve." Derek looked up into Liam's eyes. "I don't remember much. I was too young."

"Does that bother you … that you don't remember much?"

"I remember sitting on her bed—reading. I remember the day she died. When she stopped breathing. I'll remember that silence as much as I remember my mother's screams."

"How old were you in that picture?"

"Five."

"You were there when she died?"

"I was holding her hand."

Liam shook his head. "And I thought my trauma was bad. Why haven't you told me about her before now? Why did I have to be the one to bring her up?"

"Hurts too much. She was my big sister. Not a day goes by I don't think about her."

"The sadness."

"Part of it. She was so patient with me. I remember that. We would read. We would color. On days she wasn't doing as well, we would watch television tucked up in her bed."

"You have good memories of her."

Derek looked away. "I also remember her becoming more and more frail. I had to be careful. My mom was always on me about that. Be careful, Derek. She's breakable." He wiped away a tear that streaked down his cheek. "Then one morning, during a movie, she just stopped breathing."

"And you were holding her hand."

"We always held hands when we were watching television."

"She sounds like she was a very special sister."

Derek nodded. "She was."

"How long after that did you lose your parents? A year?"

"Yeah, about a year later."

"And you've never been to counseling?"

"Not my thing."

"What if I went with you?" Liam asked.

Derek studied Liam's eyes. "You would do that?"

"Of course, I would. I want to support you in any way I can."

"God, I love you." Derek swept the back of his hand across Liam's cheek.

"Love you too." Liam settled in at Derek's side. Within minutes, his breathing slowed. Derek kissed Liam's forehead. He could stay like that for an eternity, with Liam in his arms.

They walked the path up to Liam's brother's house. More like an estate in all honesty. His brother and his wife were doing well for themselves. Lucas—a lawyer. Rebecca—a surgeon.

Liam rang the doorbell and a handsome dark-haired man opened the door. He didn't have the same beauty as Liam … but then, maybe Derek was biased.

"Liam!" Lucas pulled Liam into his arms, then stepped back from the door to let them in. Derek's heart was thudding fast in his chest. This was important. These people were Liam's family. A family he wanted to be part of. He needed to fit in.

Lucas held his hand out to Derek and shook his hand.

"And you must be Derek?"

Derek smiled. "Guilty." It had slipped out. A damned legal reference. Now he felt like an idiot. His face flushed. He felt slightly better when Lucas laughed.

"Come in." Lucas led them to the kitchen. "I'm cooking chicken cordon bleu." He pointed toward a woman sipping on a glass of red wine. Long, sleek, brown hair. Impeccably dressed. Stunning eyes. "My wife Rebecca is supervising."

Derek reached for and took her hand. "Hey, I'm Derek."

"Pleasure." The handshake was firm. She wasn't the kind of person you messed with. Strength poured off her. Lucas appeared to be her counterbalance. He was laughing and joking with Liam.

"Can I get you both a drink?" Rebecca rose to her feet. "We have red and white." She looked at Liam. "Or beer and cider, if you'd prefer."

Derek's instinct was to go for a beer, but it seemed out of place in such an opulent house. He followed Liam's lead and accepted a glass of white wine.

He sat on a stool facing the immense, white marble island. He scanned the room. There were two fridges. One with a stainless front. One with a glass door. It was filled with wine and other beverages. He looked up. The ceilings had to be 12 feet, at least.

"So, did you grow up in Victoria, Derek," Lucas asked.

"Port Alberni."

"Some beautiful scenery up that way." Lucas checked the chicken through the oven door. One of three. One was smaller than the rest. Could be a warming oven.

"Liam tells me you're a bartender," Liam continued.

"Career." Derek fiddled with his wine glass. He wasn't sure why he was giving one-word answers. He suspected his nerves were getting the better of him. "Been there eighteen years."

There. Added some.

"That's commitment," Lucas answered. "You must be good at your job."

"I've won a few awards along the way."

Liam shoved Derek. "You have? I didn't know that."

"Yeah, for original signature cocktails. Stuff like that."

"Proud of you." Liam slung his arm around Derek's shoulder and kissed his cheek. "Love this man to bits."

Lucas narrowed his eyes and leaned against the island counter. He reached for Liam's left hand and touched the ring. "What's this?"

Liam grinned. "Our surprise. We were going to tell you over dinner."

"You got married?" Lucas said.

"Sort of," Derek answered. "We had a commitment ceremony. Exchanged vows."

"Wow," Rebecca said. "That's a big step."

"It was incredible," Liam said. "We took our vows in front of a campfire."

"In February," Lucas said.

"Yeah, it was a little cold," Derek replied.

"So," Lucas said. "This is *that* serious."

"Forever serious," Liam said.

Lucas's eyebrows rose and he straightened up. "I hadn't realized."

Liam frowned. "Is that a problem?"

"No … no. Nothing like that," Lucas replied. "I'm just a

bit surprised. When you said you dated men, I imagined it was just a passing thing."

Liam crossed his arms. "I'm thirty-six. That's kind of a long passing phase."

"I didn't mean to offend you," Lucas said, then looked at Derek. "Or you." He walked around to the other side of the island and put his hand on Liam's shoulder. "I'm happy for the two of you."

Liam sighed. "Thank you. You had me worried there for a moment."

Lucas patted Liam's shoulder. "Sorry. Not my intention." He walked over to the stove and lifted the lid on some steaming vegetables. "So, how does this work? Are you having kids?"

"That's a hard no," Liam replied.

"So, it'll be just the two of you."

"That's enough for us," Derek said.

"I moved into Derek's apartment yesterday," Liam said.

"You're really doing this?" Lucas propped himself against a counter.

"There's that tone again," Liam said.

Lucas shook his head. "It's just a bit for me to get my mind around. I suppose you have more in common than you would with a woman."

"That's part of it," Liam said. "I connect with men on a different level." He reached for and held Derek's hand. "And the physical stuff …. Oh, my God."

Lucas smirked. "Let's keep that part to yourself, all right?"

"We love each other," Derek said. "Everything we do together embodies that."

"We do not doubt that," Rebecca said. "We just want to make sure Liam is safe."

"We'll never be safe," Liam said. "Goes with the territory, but we're both willing to take that risk. Our love is more important than what other people might think of it."

"Liam is as safe with me as he can be," Derek said. "I would die protecting him."

"That's good enough for me," Lucas said. "I just wanted to make sure you knew what you were getting yourself into."

"I'm getting myself into a deep, enduring love," Liam said. "That's all that matters."

Lucas popped open the oven door. "Chicken is ready." He looked at Liam. "Help me serve up? Your life partner can enjoy the rest of his wine."

Derek smiled. It had been bumpy but he felt accepted.

He'd added to his growing family.

The pub was bustling. The drinks were flowing and the summer heat outside was making the interior stifling. Derek took a long swallow of his beer. This time he wasn't the ninth wheel. He was with his friends and had Liam by his side. His life partner. The only person that had ever made him feel like he wasn't alone. The feeling of something missing wasn't there anymore.

His heart was close to bursting. Liam was chatting and laughing with his friends like he'd known them all his life. Even Jackson had accepted Liam. How could he not?

He turned Liam's face to him and kissed him.

"Mmm," Liam hummed.

Derek wanted everyone to know Liam was with him.

That he was his one true love. That they had vowed to share a life. That they'd always be by each other's sides.

That their love would continue to grow.

He stroked Liam's ring.

"Love you," Liam whispered.

"I'm forever yours."

And he was.

Their story had only just begun.

Dear Reader

I hope you enjoyed reading *Capital Adoration*.

Please take a moment to review this book on the website of the store where you purchased your copy of *Capital Adoration*.

If you would like to touch base and say hello to the author, you can email them at: leigh@leighjarrett.com

About the Author

Leigh Jarrett (she/he) is an unabashedly queer, quirky, and passionate author of Contemporary MM+ Romantic Fiction. Their published contemporary works include warm and always sexy HEA romances as well as dark romances filled with grit, trauma, and angst.

In their hometown of Victoria, BC, Canada, Leigh can be found nestled up with their fabulously supportive wife and trusty laptop or enjoying the wondrous Vancouver Island outdoors.

Please consider subscribing to Leigh's newsletter to stay up to date with their new releases and promos. If you're interested in MM+ Fantasy and Paranormal Romance, check out one of Leigh's other pen names, JT Fader, on their JT Fader Fantasticals website and newsletter jtfader.com.

To connect with Leigh Jarrett:

Email: leigh@leighjarrett.com

Website and newsletter: leighjarrett.com

You can also find Leigh on Bluesky

Other Books by Leigh Jarrett

"It all came down to a matter of trust."
A Friends to Lovers M/M Gay Romance
Snowblind

"Find love in the least expected place."
An Enemies to Lovers M/M Gay Romance

Merlot Rebellion

"Brave enough to pursue love."
An Age Gap M/M Gay Romance

Pacific Pursuit

"Learning a new path to love."
A Roommates to Lovers Bisexual Awakening M/M Romance

Academic Adoration

"Recovering true love."
A Second Chance Hurt/Comfort M/M Romance

Drag Undivided

"Strumming your way to love."
A Grumpy/Sunshine Gay Awakening M/M Romance

Rhythmic Bliss